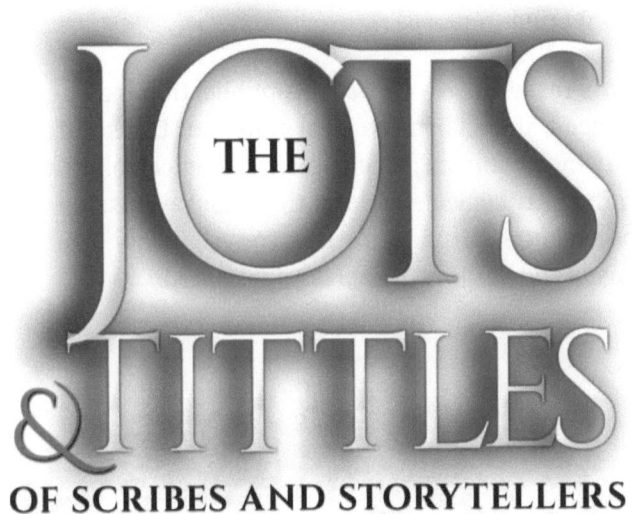

THE JOTS & TITTLES

OF SCRIBES AND STORYTELLERS

The Jots & Tittles of Scribes and Storytellers

Copyright © 2018 by MOMENTUM! Publishing
DHBonner Virtual Solutions LLC
www.dhbonner.net

ISBN: 978-0-9980734-0-8

Published in the United States of America

This book is dedicated to *Sister-hood*...

I couldn't have done this thing called life without you.

Then He said to them, *"Therefore every scribe instructed concerning the kingdom of heaven is like a householder who brings out of his treasure things new and old."*

~ *Jesus*; the ULTIMATE STORYTELLER
(Matthew 13:52)

TABLE OF CONTENTS

The Plan

... pray without ceasing,
in everything give thanks; for this is the will
of God in Christ Jesus for you."

~1 Thessalonians 5:16-18

"Today is going to be a great day – I can just feel it", Jurnee said, as she smiled and began her morning prayer – *"Lord, thank you for today. Thank you for this opportunity and for all the gifts you have given me. I know you have my best interest at heart... and I trust you. I know that you are just and that you will give me victory.*

Amen."

"Therefore I tell you,
whatever you ask in prayer,
believe that you have received it,
and it will be yours."

~Mark 11:24

Jurnee had a meeting scheduled with her boss, and the President of the company, for later that morning. The previous week they had informed her that the meeting was very important; but, provided no other information.

Over the years, Jurnee had presented at workshops and conferences, on both a local and state level, for the organization.

She represented them well; receiving numerous awards for her efforts. So, she knew this meeting was going to be the day they would tell her – *Great job!* This was the recognition she had been longing for, and since receiving the meeting request, now greatly anticipated.

... and, for your achievements and loyalty, we want to offer you a promotion.

Jurnee could already hear the company President's words in her heart; easily picturing her new office in great detail, while thrilled about the potential for increased travel opportunities beyond the States.

Though a bit anxious, Jurnee was excited about this meeting, because it was going to be another milestone in her career - to put her on a platform to continue in her personal development; as well as, being a contributor to the development of those around her.

See, as a young child, she had envisioned herself being in a position, and having a career, that would give her the ability to impact the lives of others for the better. Jurnee wanted to help young ladies, who were presented with challenges or struggles, to understand that it was all temporary and that they could overcome.

She also wanted to help young boys and men to feel proud of their sisters, mothers, grandmothers and aunts; to have a sense of pride in what they were doing and in what they could, and would, one day become.

Once she became a young adult, Jurnee had begun to contemplate the "HOW"... *how* she could help others get to their next level, *how* she could help them grow, and *how* she could support their development. She believed in this mission so deeply, that she was fully convinced this promotion would act as the yellow brick road that would pave the way for her to serve others.

She arrived to the conference room ten minutes before the appointed time, and sat down. Slowly looking around the room, she took in all of the employee pictures and achievement plaques, pausing at the space which held the frame with her image and the awards inscribed with her name, *Jurnee Love.*

Soon, the digital clock on the wall across from her registered on the hour, and the sound of footsteps and voices could be heard coming down the hall toward her. Within a moment, two older white men – the president and her boss - entered the conference room door.

Jurnee stood to greet them, yet quickly noticed that both of them were expressionless; not their usual friendly selves.

THE PLAN

The president stood tall, with his head nearly touching the ceiling, causing Jurnee to feel about 2 inches small. Yet, she was determined that nothing would shake her drive and confidence, because today was HER day.

"Good morning," she said, with her best smile.

Neither man returned her greeting.

"Jurnee, thank you for coming, but I am afraid I have a bit of bad news," the tall slinky-looking man stated, without emotion.

"The organization is going in a different direction. We are restructuring and your position is being eliminated; therefore, your employment and benefits will end today. We do appreciate all that you have done for the company, and in your department, especially. I do hope that things will work out for you, as I believe that you have a great future ahead of you. You are talented and you have a caring and giving heart.

I'm sorry.

Please clear out your desk and office immediately."

Her boss said nothing. He simply leaned over, reached out his right hand, and shook hers.

In that moment, there was total silence – her world stood still. It had happened again! It had happened AGAIN! It had happened.... again? In shock, Jurnee's stomach began to ache and her heart started pounding loud and hard. Immediately, she was filled with a bitter mixture of disappointment, anger, sadness, and emptiness.

After taking a long, slow, deep breath, Jurnee looked the taller man in his eyes, smiled, extended her hand, and quietly said, *"I appreciate your time and thank you for the opportunity. It has been a pleasure working here."* She walked out the office with her head held high.

It was only five minutes after the hour.

Once she had gathered her personal things from her desk, she left the building and got into her car. She had been able to drive out of the parking lot, around the corner, and to the first traffic light on the next street, before it happened; that feeling from before returned.

But this time, it was amplified and unrestrained.

"Why?!" she screamed in rage.

Sitting at the light, the tears began flowing like a river. She had given her all in this job, just like she had given her all in her marriage. And, in the same way, Jurnee had awakened one day and everything had changed. These men in her life, for no apparent reason or explanation, just decided to change their minds.

After the car behind her honked to alert her that the light had turned green, Jurnee came back to herself.

Slowly turning left onto the street she had driven down for the past ten years as she made her way to and from the office, she wiped her tears and tried to concentrate on the road.

Still, her soul was broken.

Did she not believe enough in the prayers she prayed daily? Why had the past decade been such a constant rollercoaster ride: UP, and DOWN, and BUMPY? Being jerked here and there – not able to stand and being fearful of climbing the hills that lead to the next level or milestone in her life.

"Why?!" she screamed again. *"Lord, please tell me why? Help me to understand! God, you said that you would not allow anything in my life I could not handle, but I need you to help me now! God, I need you to help me on this journey – because I am feeling super weak. I am tired."*

She pulled into her driveway and turned off the car. As she sat there, she began to wonder about her name. Understanding that with a name like "Jurnee", there would be journeys in life, but why were there so many tornadoes and hurricanes and tsunamis along the way? Why so many mountains to climb? Why not cruises in the ocean or flights to paradise lands? Why not a journey that was more refreshing; one that allowed her a moment to exhale, live life, and love?

Jurnee shook her head.

Everything she had done – all that hard work – had it all been in vain? Could it be that God was taking a break from the blessing business? Did God not remember what He said, what He promised; that He would protect her and work all things out for those who love Him?

What was really going on?

Having gotten out of the car, Jurnee turned the key in the lock of her home, and went inside.

THE PLAN

"Therefore if any man be in Christ,
he is a new creature: old things are passed away;
behold, all things are become new.

~2 Corinthians 5:17

A little about Jurnee.

Seven years ago, she had made a vow of celibacy and told God she would wait for the man HE would send her. She made the commitment to focus more on God and live out her purpose; reading her bible more, attending church and bible study, and asking questions, whenever there was doubt or a lack of understanding. She gave thanks every morning before she got out of bed, every night before she went to bed, and even multiple times during the day.

She had made a vow to make a change.

She decided to change who she was; declaring that the new and improved person she was going to be, would be so phenomenal – Jurnee 2.0.

Her caramel, mocha brown, smooth skin was free from blemishes or spots; her smile displayed perfectly-shaped, pearly white teeth. She had been graced with features that had given her opportunities to model when she was younger – she had even been featured in a few commercials.

Wanting to declare the change she had made in her life, Jurnee did the big chop. Her short natural hair was a combination of curly and kinky texture. She would frequently wear blow out styles, rod curl styles, and twists.

Jurnee walked with grace and dignity, pride, and energy. Standing naturally at 5 feet 2 inches tall, she had an obsession for shoes; pumps, open toed, canvas sneakers, sandals, or boots. You name it, Jurnee had dedicated a closet just for her shoes. She could also be seen in dresses, dress pants, or suits on any given day, as she loved to dress business or business casual. She had her moments when she wore sweats, but it was not very often. She also loved to wear sweet and flowery smelling perfumes.

But... who is Jurnee, now?

THE PLAN

Today, she is an African American woman with a broken heart and a will that has been lost. She is the one who will be your friend, even when those she thought were her friends began to play "hide and seek". And now, she couldn't find anyone who would listen to her, comfort her, or even try to understand that things were different for her now.

For the first few hours after arriving home, she tried calling a few of them, only to be greeted with voicemails and text messages that read, *let me get back with you*, or hurried whispers of *let me call you back tomorrow.*

Today, she was ALONE.

The feelings from earlier began to creep back on the scene; tip-toeing like they wanted to startle her – catch her off guard *again*. She cried out *"Lord, help deliver me from this feeling of NOT... Not able, not loved, not attractive, not smart, not worth anything. God, I don't know how, but I know you will do it – whatever it is."*

No job, because they had just fired her, even though Jurnee had helped the company gain clients, exposure, and even unpredicted revenue. No man, because her husband conveniently forgot his promise to never hurt her. Somehow that promise had slipped his mind when he began to abuse her emotionally, mentally, and physically.

No potential romantic interest, because of her vow of celibacy. No other man seemed to want to wait with her; instead, they came with an agenda and *waiting* was not on the list.

No support from friends, because the ones she thought were her friends, had only been there when they could get something out of the relationship.

And, no 'will', because all of her determination, motivation, and energy had been stolen - kidnapped and held ransom with nothing and no one there willing to help pay the price.

Mentally fatigued from the events of the day, Jurnee crawled into bed, let the tears fall, and eventually fell asleep.

THE PLAN

"What does it profit, my brethren, if someone says
he has faith but does not have works?
Can faith save him?"

~James 2:14

Early the next morning, Jurnee awakened, and said a prayer as she did every day... *Lord, thank you for today. Thank you for this opportunity to make an IMPACT in the life of someone today. Thank you for all the gifts you have given me. I know you have my best interest at heart and I trust you. I know that you are just and that you will give me victory.*

But this morning - the very next morning - was already presenting itself as another hard pill to swallow. Jurnee still did not want to face reality. So, in an attempt to change her mindset and think positive, she continued to speak the words of her prayer, despite the tears filling her eyes and running down her cheek... *Lord, thank you! The meeting happened. It was a door closing, and I know you have an even bigger door that you will open. I trust you, God. And, I know that it all will work out when the time is right and YOU say so.*

Amen.

As she lay there, Jurnee recalled a pastor saying that faith without works is dead. So, she got out the bed, washed her face, and got dressed. Sitting down at the desk in her home office, Jurnee began to conduct job searches, make phone calls, and get the word out that she was available for new opportunities and accepting clients for her business.

Between multiple refills of hot tea, she shared on her Facebook page, her Twitter and Instagram pages, and her LinkedIn status. As the day progressed, she enlisted a college student to upgrade her website, while soliciting assistance from a local Human Resources professional to assist with the new look of her resume.

Jurnee got through the day by keeping busy.

One day turned into the next, and Jurnee took the time to not only look for work, but also to invest in herself. She got her hair and nails done, bought a few new outfits, and had a makeover done at the local mall; consistently praying and asking God to reveal how she could strengthen and renew her faith.

To that end, she decided to volunteer at homeless shelters, domestic violence shelters, and some of the nonprofits in the area. She began to pray with *and for* the people in the shelters.

This, because, she realized she needed to not get stuck in her own situation; mourning what she had lost. She knew that by helping others who were less fortunate, she could retain perspective and a deeper appreciation for what she had left – her house, car, food, etc.

Throughout the following weeks and months, her faith was continually renewed, because she became grateful for being able to wake up in a bed. That she had clothes to wear. And, that when she opened the refrigerator and the cabinets in the kitchen, she had all the food she needed. Things weren't as bad as they seemed. And no, God hadn't taken a vacation from the blessing business.

She was indeed blessed!

Jurnee thought, *Is it possible that I'm the one who has taken a break from blessing others, because I've been so comfortable and focused on myself?*

In that moment, she decided to turn the page and begin a new chapter in her life. Soon after, she became even more acutely aware of God's presence in the EVERYDAY.

It seemed that He would send signs, and little reminders, in something as simple as a few social media posts:

"You are enough"
-Unknown

She heard a whisper - *Love yourself!* No need for a man to validate you. No need to allow family to manipulate you. No need for feelings of being without value, without love, without beauty. *You are enough.*

Being a survivor of domestic violence and reflecting on the past, Jurnee began to truly feel the importance of these words and how they can impact your life. She began to fully understand that God has given her all the tools she needed to endure it all – whatever *"it"* is.

THE PLAN

**"No one can make you feel inferior
without your permission"**
-Eleanor Roosevelt

She began to praise God, because even though she had been brought up in dysfunction, she was now being delivered from it. With a convicted heart, Jurnee started journaling to get all the negative feelings out, and made a promise to herself to leave them in that book; no longer dwelling on them. The "pity party" had to be over... it must be over. All the guests had to leave the building: resentment, anger, sorrow, worry, and fear.

She had experienced being *in the moment* with them, but now she needed to allow God to do what He does best, and that is take care of His children.

**"When you feel like quitting,
think about why you started."**
-Unknown

Jurnee thought to herself, *yeah - God and I have this relationship. He allows me to be me, but only for a short time, and then he reminds me to let it go – so I can continue to grow.*

"The LORD himself will fight for you.
Just stay calm."

~Exodus 14:14

"I do what I do for my children. I want them to know that they can break that chain of the cycle of poverty," Jurnee said softly, as she lay on her bed with her back against the headboard and her laptop opened on the lap pad seated next to her. She was filling out more applications, while taking sips of a mildly-brewed peppermint flavored tea, from her favorite mug that her daughter gave her with the words 'You are my SHERO'.

Jurnee became lost in thought. Completing her degrees was for them. Buying a house was for them. Traveling, and going on vacation, was for them. She had had none of these things growing up, and she was very grateful that God had afforded her the opportunity to provide them for her children; so that they could experience them.

The truth is that I do what I do, to be a testimony to God's goodness, grace, and mercy. So that I can help the next one – to pay it forward.

She remembered a poem she had written a few years before; sharing with a community of women entitled, "*Matters of the Heart*". She had challenged the ladies to really think about what mattered to them; what were the matters of their hearts?: Relationships lost and found, family (the good and bad), past and present work, joy for what makes them happy, being thankful about what gives them peace, doing what they love - with who they love, believing in themselves – even when faced with challenges, and trusting GOD for everything... including their dreams.

Embrace it all; because all of it really does matter.

Suddenly, it hit her. *It does matter.*

Wow! It does matter that she lost the job, because she found her strength; strength to get out of bed, even when she didn't want to, strength to smile in adversity, strength to keep going and not look back, because there is nothing for her in the rear-view mirror.

Her destiny is not tied to the past.

It does matter that she was misused and mistreated by men in her life, because she found her worth – her self-worth; her value. And no, it does not change based on someone's inability to recognize how much of a jewel she was. Jurnee thought, *shame on them for not seeing what God sees in me. It truly is their loss.*

It does matter that no one told her she was cute growing up, because now she had found her beauty; a beauty that was so deep – it showed, not only on the outside, but also from the inside... a beauty that was not just an adjective to describe her outward appearance, but an expression of who she really was.

It does matter that she now had an understanding of how to appreciate life and all that it offered; understanding the value of hugs, and kisses, and the words 'I love you'.

Jurnee now fully comprehended that time was precious and should never be taken for granted. She was learning to forgive more and love more deeply. Not to put off for tomorrow what should be, could be, done today.

THE PLAN

And yes, it does matter that she kept her promise; continuing to wait for the one God has prepared for her!

As she took another sip of her now cold tea, Jurnee heard a small voice whisper, *"And whenever you stand praying, forgive, if you have anything against anyone, so that your Father also who is in heaven may forgive you for your trespasses."*

Jurnee paused, mid-sip, and carefully set the mug back onto the nightstand. *Am I still holding onto anger? Have I truly moved on?*

And, then... she found that place called forgiveness.

Her Son's Father: She forgave him for telling her son that he wasn't the father, that his mother was a whore, and all the other lies he told that her son believed because he wanted a relationship with his father. She forgave him for not taking the DNA test that would put any doubt to rest. She forgave him for that time when she was pregnant and he cheated on her with another woman; getting her pregnant too.

She forgave him for not coming to any football games, or auditions, or talent shows, even though he lived less than 15 minutes away. She forgave him for not realizing how wonderful, beautiful, and talented a son they had. She forgave him for not wanting to provide financial support and not being there in any other way.

Her Mother: She forgave her mother for admitting that she never loved her, and for telling her that she wished she had never been born. She forgave her for telling her that she never hugged her, because she was not gay, so there was no need to hug her; that Jurnee just needed to get out of her feelings. She forgave her mother for opening multiple accounts in her name and for the credit she had to repair because of this.

She forgave her mother for making her feel less than.... less than perfect, less than pretty or beautiful, less than smart, less than worthy, less than loved. She forgave her for not understanding that Jurnee had a son and that he was not a replacement for the son her mother had lost.

Yes, her mother resented her because her brother had died. And, although Jurnee tried to instill discipline in her son and motivate him to do something besides hang in the streets, her mother told him that he could do whatever he wanted; even introducing him to drugs, rather than encouraging him to go to school and break the cycle that had been in the family for many years; the cycle of the men either being dead or going to jail.

She forgave her mother when her son tried to kill himself - and she needed her mother to take the time out to give Jurnee encouragement, guidance, strength, and hope. Yet, while Jurnee's son was in the hospital, her mother said she was too busy to come see him; making the decision to go shopping instead.

Her Son: When she escaped the death of her son when he tried to commit suicide- she forgave him; knowing he had struggled mentally for reasons she could not even fathom. He often told her that he hated her and that he did a lot of what he did to hurt her on purpose. He admitted that many times he did this because his grandmother had told him to do it.

Nevertheless, she tried her best to sow seeds of self-respect, discipline, and self-love; telling him daily that she loved him. So, for all the times he had lashed out at her, no matter the reason, she forgave him.

For the Men in Her Life: To the ones who broke her heart, cheated on her, shattered her dreams, belittled her accomplishments, and were just plain MEAN... She forgave them. She forgave the ones who told her she was beautiful or smart just to have their way with her. She forgave the ones who raped her mind, spirit, and love.

She especially forgave the one who had physically raped her, resulting in a pregnancy; loving the child, despite the method of conception. She knew she had to learn to forgive because the anger and negativity was only hurting her. She was the only one who didn't sleep well at night thinking of it all. She forgave herself for being young and naïve... and she forgave him.

She forgave them all and then... she forgave herself for giving herself to any of them. She forgave herself for thinking she wasn't worthy of anything, or anyone, better; thinking she deserved to be raped because she had done BAD things in the past. She forgave herself for blaming herself and thinking that anything negative was because she deserved to be punished. This, surprisingly, was extremely difficult to do.

It wasn't easy, but she did it.

THE PLAN

SHE FORGAVE HERSELF!

Her Father: And, then... she forgave her father for the molestation in her early years of life. She forgave her father for not coming to any of her singing, dance, or cheer competitions, awards, assemblies, graduations, or birth of any of her children.

She forgave him for not BEING – for not being that model or living example of what a man should do or how a man should act. She had repeatedly told him that she needed a father, but accepted that time could not be rewound.

Jurnee began to reflect on a poem she had written to him years before, when she had long ago began her journey of forgiveness:

A little girl needs her father.

A grown woman does too

I really wish our relationship was different

I wish I had the chance to get to know you

As a child, I needed to know how to love and not lust

And when giving myself to him

I must

DR. JOY LOUGH

First trust

And believe in myself

and just be

sure that he was worth me

you see that's what I needed....

From you

I needed to know when to just "like"

A little girl needs to know how to win when she fights

She needs to know when to let go

And when to keep go–ing

To pursue her dreams

I wish just one time you heard me sing

I wish you had a connection with your grandchildren

I wish you were there when

My son played football,

Or when my daughter danced

I wish they knew you

I wish you would have given them the chance

That I didn't have

You see since you weren't there

I didn't have anyone to show me

or tell me

THE PLAN

or guide me

So, lucky me

Or maybe just dummy me

I found someone just like you

someone who ran from his responsibilities

And now my children feel exactly like I do

Wondering how it would have been different

Wondering if daddy even cares

Wondering if it is something that they did

The reason he is not there

You see no birthday or Christmas card or even phone call

Really scars a child – it leaves a huge void

And even as an adult sometimes I get extremely

Annoyed

Because I am not sure if I can heal

And I'm not really sure what to feel

or even how to feel

For you

I know that life doesn't always go as planned

And even with your continued absence

DR. JOY LOUGH

I pray for understanding

And I know that you are still my father

And I must love you

because God asked me to

and because it's the right thing to do

but please know that I really did and do miss you

talent shows

games

multiple degrees

you were a no show

with all the accomplishments

the desire was still there

and made me want YOU there

even more

But before my life has come to an end

I just want you to know…And the whole world too

That I forgive you!

And most of all

In spite of it all

DADDY, I DO LOVE YOU!

And Yes – I forgive you!

THE PLAN

She forgave him.

There was this nagging voice pulling at her telling her not to forgive, that nothing would come of it, but she did it anyway.

She forgave them all *and* she forgave herself.

*"She is clothed with strength and dignity,
and she laughs without fear of the future.
When she speaks, her words are wise, and
she gives instructions with kindness."*

~Proverbs 31:25

The next few days turned into weeks, and then those weeks turned into several months. Jurnee would continue to wake up with a grateful heart. Each day feeling more passionate, determined, and trusting than the day before.

Every morning, she would say, *"Lord thank you for today. Thank you for this opportunity to make an IMPACT in the life of someone today. Thank you for all the gifts you have given me. I know you have my best interest at heart and I trust you. I know that you are just and that you will give me victory.*

Amen."

THE PLAN

One Tuesday morning, around 10am, her phone rang. It was a job offer that she had not even applied for!

Somehow, her contact information and history had been forwarded to the company; probably from one of her social media posts. A stern, yet feminine, voice introduced herself and the reason for the call. The young lady then shared the expectations for the position, asking Jurnee a few preliminary questions.

After Jurnee responded, the voice immediately asked, *"Ms. Love, will you be able to come in today for an interview?"*

Jurnee had figured it out – THE PLAN.

God revealed that the plan for her life, the purpose of her life, was to share her story with others; to encourage others who have gone through, or were going through, what she had experienced. The plan was to speak life to those who felt that their dreams, goals, or desires had an expiration date. The plan was to smile and be grateful for it all, because it all shall be well.

Later that same day, Jurnee walked into yet another conference room; standing tall. And, with every step, she projected strength and courage; radiating such confidence that you had to take a second look. However, this time, her trust wasn't in any outward display of what she had accomplished... no pictures on the walls; no plaques, no awards.

Just the smile she wore, as she exuded her faith in God and the knowledge of who she was in Him.

The interview began, with the panel of five deliberating briefly, then asking, *"Why should we hire you?"*

"You should hire me, because I am an expert at what I do. I am skilled at speaking, teaching, and delivering results. I am a motivator and I am motivated.

I am determined and will persevere in the vilest conditions.

It is essential that I be here. Not just to fill a position, but to help excel the company's bottom line, as well as promote growth and development to everyone that I meet."

Jurnee smiled. It was the closer.

It was all a part of... THE PLAN!

The Color of Character

PROLOGUE

This is a Man's World

✼

As I maneuvered my way through the congested city traffic and settled into the flow on the expressway for my long drive home, I hit the repeat button and pumped up the volume on Etta James' rendition of an ole James Brown song, *This is a Man's World*.

The song was not a part of my "usual" cruising down the road joints, but it was on the compilation CD included in a wonderful gift box from my best friend and old college roommate Samantha. Sam presented it to me the last night of our stay as I was packing for my return trip home.

THE COLOR OF CHARACTER

I was deeply touched by all of the contents that filled the beautifully packaged gift; including the selection of songs on the CD. It was obvious that she had put much thought and care into it because each item held great significance in relation to our bond, or something we had just shared. She had managed to make purchases and then create this wonderful expression of love, during our time together, and without me even being aware.

Sam and I had maintained a close relationship over the years; so, there was very little, if anything, happening in our lives that the other was not fully aware of (until now). We communicated regularly and our families came together for extended visits during the summer and on certain holidays throughout the year; but it was a rarity that she and I got to spend any time together separate from our husbands and children.

However, there had been so much transpiring in my world since our last visit that I knew a face-to-face, one-on-one conclave was in order; not to mention, that the delicacy of some of the subject matter I needed to discuss would not translate well over the phone, nor in the company of anyone else.

ELAINE ROUNDTREE MONTFORD

There was one subject in particular I wasn't quite sure how to broach – not even with Sam. But I knew if I was going to share it at all, it would most definitely be with her. If she couldn't handle it, there wasn't a snowball's chance in the Sahara that anyone else could. So, we planned a 'sister sabbatical' and met at her and Demetrius' (her husband) vacation home; just the two of us.

Normally I would have hopped a flight and been there in little or no time, but this time I had decided to drive down so that I could use the time to decompress and clear my head; attempting to devise a strategy of how I would share my life-altering news with my dearest friend. I could not remember a time or subject matter that I had struggled so hard to share. She was without a doubt, my closest friend and confidante, and we shared EVERYTHING with each other; so why was I in such turmoil with this particular one?

I guess my fear was that even she wouldn't believe me. I could just hear her saying, "My Lawd from Zion... it's finally happened! You have let them folk crack the last egg in yo basket. Michael bout to have yo behind committed – and if he don't, I will!"

THE COLOR OF CHARACTER

Truth be told, if I wasn't experiencing it, I would not believe it my own self. I kept asking myself, "Self, am I crazy?" My self would usually respond, "I don't know, but it kind of feels like it to me – the mere fact that you're talking to yourself while anticipating an answer that you don't already know (because YOU are answering); *Hmmm*, I'd say that qualifies you to be just a little suspect, if you're asking me… and you did ask me right?"

At any rate, I had finally settled on a method, and had practically convinced myself that it would work. That is, until I saw her… and I was filled with complete uncertainty all over again.

We spent the majority of our time those ten days, relaxing, reminiscing, and playing catch-up. We talked about our college days shenanigans, our husbands and their idiosyncrasies, the state of our marriages, our children and their craziness, our careers, including our colleagues and their drama; and of course, the state of our crazy, mixed up world in general.

We shared our ideas on everything from how to cure the world's ills, to how to prepare the world's best mac and cheese. We laughed and cried; danced and drank our favorite wine until we both fell fast asleep – this basically became our nightly routine.

And so far, my secret was still safe.

During the evening sharing session about our husbands and our marriage, I shared how my marriage was on the brink of divorce. I tearfully disclosed how devastated I was when I stopped by Michael's office dressed to the nines, to surprise him and take him to dinner at our favorite restaurant, but walked in on him and his secretary in the throes of passionate lovemaking.

I told her how I thought that had been the pinnacle of our marital discord, but how Michael had shared in one of our mediation sessions that he had felt us drifting apart long before that occurred; and that he felt our relationship was emotionally and intimately dissolved long before we reached the point of his infidelity.

Through my sobs, I shared how in our last session he angrily spewed that he felt I had shown more interest in my career and new promotion than I did in him, our marriage, our daughter, or anything else; and he felt like he couldn't compete with my new love. He admitted that the affair with his secretary was wrong, but that in a moment of weakness, he had given in.

I readily confessed to her that I had become super vigilant in regard to work... almost paranoid about being able to maintain my new position in lieu of all the back-biting and underhanded schemes I had witnessed going on amongst my colleagues on a regular basis; so, I felt the need to remain watchful and proactive in order to protect myself. Though I refused to consider it then, maybe I had made that my top priority.

I reiterated to her that my greatest fear had always been feeling that I couldn't measure up; and I added that lately, I felt like that fear had finally materialized. Despite how my life may have looked to others, it felt like an utter failure to me; and Michael's adulterous behavior was just the proverbial straw that broke the camel's back. I openly questioned whether everything that I was working so hard to secure, had not been just a facade; and now it was all about to disintegrate bit by bit.

Now Sam was never one to hold her tongue, or try to temper her words or her emotions – she was high-spirited, straightforward, and unwavering; and could sometimes be brutally honest. She never left to chance what she meant in regard to anything. But I had grown to love and respect her honesty.

So, I took it to heart when she said that I could sometimes be a donkey because I became overly obsessed with trying to be perfect; and that obviously, I was still wrestling with knowing the difference between Perfection and Excellence. The fact that she had already consumed more than her fair share of alcohol that evening seemed to help loosen her tongue, and she didn't hold back; she fired at me with both barrels.

"I never pegged you to be a slow learner, but Honey, you may need a remedial course in Self Esteem. First of all, I don't know why it's so important for you to gain the approval of the whole world anyway! Why are you still shadowboxing with ghosts from your past? I understand that you want to be seen as worthy. Hell... we all do to some degree.

However, I am not worried about those from back in the day who spoke 'gloom and doom over me', nor am I concerned about those in the present who have no say or control over me and my affairs. Why? Because I am confident in myself - whether I have a dollar or a million dollars, the money don't make me... I make the money; and them same fools who were talking smack back then, are trying to borrow a dollar from me now!

Everyone, BUT you, seems to be able to recognize your worth. What is it going to take for you to see it? You've spent most of your life trying to prove everybody wrong, and you have made some amazing things happen in your life so far. But all the stuff you've acquired loses its meaning if you don't believe you deserve it.

The educational degrees, the prestigious career, the mansion on the hill, the luxurious automobiles, the perfect family, the designer clothes... all of it becomes nothing more than merit badges whose weight can seem unbearable if there's not a foundation of confidence and truth to support them. And, without a solid foundation, they hang like chains shackled to your soul that will slowly rip it to shreds.

If you're not really careful, you'll wind up spending half your life accumulating all these status symbols, and the other half of your life defending your right to have them. If you don't believe you deserve it, they won't have to take them from you – you'll relinquish them all by default.

So, as I see it, it's not whether or not 'they' think you're worthy... the question is, do *you* think you're worthy? To be perfectly honest with you, I really don't give a flying fig what 'they' think about you or me. I do however, care about you. Now you know, I will hurt anybody who even looks at you wrong my sister! PFFFT - you knooow I don't play when it comes to that! And that includes that %$&* bonehead husband of yours!

Speaking of which – *what the what* is Michael's problem? Even IF you had lost your focus for a minute, that does not justify him losing his mind! There's no excuse for that!"

Sam had shifted gears and moved from lecturing me about self-worth, to screaming about Michael and his secretary... all in one fluid motion. She yelled and cursed and called Michael every name in the book. She threatened to show up at his office one day with her baseball bat and commence to swinging on him and his secretary.

We both laughed ourselves to tears at the mere thought of that, and at the mental image of a news reporter standing outside of the county jail, reporting on her arrest.

We shared all of that, and yet I still could not bring myself to broach the one subject that I was truly terrified to share.

THE COLOR OF CHARACTER

I tried to make myself initiate the conversation before she asked, but I could never muster up enough courage. So finally, the next evening, Sam asked the question I had been dreading...

You know I can feel you right?

That evening, we had enjoyed a delightful meal that we prepared together; then she shooed me out of the kitchen, refusing to allow me to assist with the clean-up. As I sat on the balcony that overlooked the lake, I closed my eyes and drifted into deep thought, replaying previous scenes from days passed, and contemplating how I would explain the unexplainable.

After finishing her kitchen cleaning detail, she silently slid into the chaise lounge beside me and gently whispered, "Danni, you do know I can feel you, right? What are you trying so hard *not* to tell me? This is me, Sam; and you should know by now that you don't have to be afraid to talk to me about anything,

Is it Michael? Is it Justice? Whatever it is, I promise you Sis, we will deal with it together."

I opened my eyes and sat silently as tears stained my cheeks. She didn't push. She reached over and brushed the tears away; then, she just sat, and waited. Once I composed myself, I began to recount what I had experienced over those past weeks, and how my entire perception of life had shifted because of my experiences.

I shared my fear of how this thing had affected every fiber of my life and how it had the potential to not only destroy everything I have labored so hard to achieve, but how, if I didn't handle it properly, it could literally destroy me.

I told her that I had not even shared it with Michael yet... that she was the first; and that I even had trepidations about sharing with her.

I expected her to go into another cursing jag, or come back with something sensationally silly or sarcastic to make me laugh and take my mind off of the subject; because that was what she would normally do when things got too heavy.

Much to my surprise, she did neither.

She reminded me that neither of our lives had been without great challenges, and that even from our childhood, we had experienced arduous journeys. But that it was those very struggles that had instilled a level of tenacity within us that prepared us to battle the formidable opponents that awaited us in our future; and that our future was now right before us.

She spoke of how we had recognized early on that the scales of justice seemed unfairly weighted to tilt in favor of others; but that it had never stopped us from excelling and carving out a niche for ourselves. She spoke of how we had both fought and clawed our way to the top; and had chosen a career that allowed us to sway those scales and bring some sense of justice not just to ourselves, but to other victims and their families.

She repeated her grandmother's ideology that had been commemorated in that James Brown R & B hit, "This is a man's world." She laughed as she quoted her Grandma Ida - "What's my take on it? This may be a man's world, but it would be a helluva mess without a woman's influence!" Sam said, "Grandma Ida may have missed the mark on some stuff, but she doggone got that one right!"

Sam sat quietly for a moment and contemplated the news I had just shared. She took my hand and offered me a benevolent smile as she conceded that she had never experienced what I had described. She said that she had always stood firm on her personal belief that if it couldn't be proven and documented in black and white, then it didn't exist.

She went on to say that she relinquished that stance over time, because she had since witnessed some things that now caused her to disavow her original conviction. She told me how Life had recently taught her that just because 'You' may not have personally experienced it, does not devalue a thing's validity.

She concluded her dialogue that evening by saying, "I know your experiences don't make any sense right now, but, just trust your heart Danni. I've learned that our heart holds truths that our mind can never fathom. There's a reason why you were given this. Just know that no matter what - I've got your back."

And with that, she smiled, reached over and hugged and kissed me, and went back inside; leaving me to quietly ponder her advice.

The last few days of our stay were even more comforting than the first; and when Sam presented me with her gift, I was overcome with emotion.

As I packed my car to leave the next morning, I left still filled with more questions than answers; but the weight of it was less oppressive because I knew that I was not alone on this portion of my journey.

Now I was headed home to share the news with my family. They would either join Sam's stance while supporting me, or they would shake their head in disbelief and walk away; but I could not allow fear to keep me in a state of limbo any longer.

It was time to find out...

I.

This is Where it All Began

✲

"We spend our whole life searching for all the things we think
we want, never really knowing what we have."
-Unknown

What you just read were actual events that happened very recently; however, there was a series of significant events which precipitated the need for that sabbatical.

Allow me to take you back to that pivotal point.

This is the story that completely changed my perception of people, of my own self, and of life.

THE COLOR OF CHARACTER

For seven years, I had labored extensively in the State Attorney's office, with a very high ratio of wins vs. losses to my credit. My dedication and passion for my profession motivated me to excel significantly.

In fact, I had just been promoted from a support staff attorney, to Executive Assistant District Attorney, with aspirations of one day becoming the D.A. This recent promotion had garnered me a certain level of respect from not only my colleagues, but from the legal community over all.

Ironically, it had also created an even greater rift in my already rocky marriage and home life. So much so, that in our last marital mediation session, my husband had vehemently accused me of caring more about my "precious career" than I did for my family… or anything else for that matter.

Sadly, as I reflect on his accusation, as much as I would have loved to argue the absurdity of it, his charge held more validity than I cared to admit at that time.

So, like my marriage, my glowing professional reputation was in danger of disintegrating right before my eyes. Truth be told, I felt the full weight of my career resting squarely on my shoulders every time I stepped foot in the office, or assumed the responsibility of lead counsel on a case, or did anything that focused attention in my direction; and even more so because of the new position.

I had been in this game long enough to become fully aware that with every advancement I achieved, there would be an even greater degree of scrutiny deliberately launched against seemingly my every move, whether on or off the job, because I was a woman in a male-dominated arena; and a minority woman to boot.

It was sad that in a world as rapidly progressive as ours, there are still some who feel entitled to certain privileges and positions based solely on their skin color or gender, while others are constantly under microscopic view to prove themselves to be marginally worthy of consideration.

I knew that in order for me to maintain my position, I had to strive to always present my 'A' game; so, I made it my business to do just that.

Over time, I began to assimilate the volatility of the pathway that led to what we deemed to be success; and I realized the price some players were willing to pay to achieve it. This was a high-stakes, winner-take-all game, and some were willing to sell their souls just to lay claim to the title of "Hot-shot", "Boy or Girl Wonder", or "The Golden Child"; all of which were indicative of one's #15 Minutes of Fame, and would prove to be very temporary, as the tagline suggests.

Yes, I learned how quickly one could move from rising star to obscurity in just the blink of an eye.

But along the way, I also gained a working knowledge of the ruthlessness of these players; even those who camouflaged themselves behind fake smiles.

No matter how much they feigned comradery, or how many of them lined the team bench - at the end of the day, I was cognizant that most of them viewed this game as a mano-a-mano/hand-to-hand combat sport; and it seemed that whoever held the coveted title became the targeted one... And so, it was crystal clear that for the moment, I was the reigning champ and thus, their chief opponent.

My move from a cubicle space to an actual office did not come without struggle or strategy; and my strategic plan to succeed had served me well. I had gleaned the ability to acquire their cunning skills, and when coupled with my innate drive to survive, it gave me the advantage I needed without having to compromise my standards by incorporating their vicious nature, or succumbing to some of their unscrupulous tactics.

The one thing that seemed to accentuate the bitter taste of envy and jealousy on their palates was that I managed to accomplish all of this with a smile, and without appearing to break a sweat.

This served to infuriate and confuse most of them to no end. But, unbeknownst to any of them, I was busy fighting my own private battles, and warring with my own weapon-wielding demons. Unlike them, I simply chose to keep my private matters private. I didn't share the details with them, nor did I seek their counsel.

My plan seemed to be working well... until it wasn't working as planned any more.

II

Court Date

Despite the multiplicity of dreadful dilemmas vying for first place on my list of priorities, I managed to show up for court that particular day in my usual fashion - impeccably dressed, adorned with flawless makeup, and not a hair out of place.

Now if I could just slow my brain down enough to focus, I might be assured of adding another mark in my win column. Or, considering my level of stress at that juncture, at the very least, display the ability to articulate and connect a chain of coherent sentences.

ELAINE ROUNDTREE MONTFORD

Elliott Prescott, who was third in the chain of command in the State Attorney's office (immediately following my position, which coincidently he was secretly conspiring to take), was co-counsel on this case and had presented our opening statement. Although it was pretty much an open and shut case, it did require me to at least 'appear' to be mentally present, so that we could present the incriminating evidence our team had worked so diligently to compile, and then subsequently, we would hear and proceed to disassemble opposing counsel's defense.

I was fairly confident that we were prepared to win this case, provided Elliott opened well, and he had; and provided I could remain adequately focused to complete the summation. But at that point, it was still early in the proceedings and I was really struggling to stay present; let alone focused.

As the defense presented their opening statement, I attempted to jot down a couple of points to address once we had our turn again, but the moment I began to write, not only did I forget what I was writing, I lost track of what was currently being said. It was not at all uncommon for me to multitask, in fact, that was more the norm than not, since the demand for my time, attention and expertise seemed to be greatly disproportionate to the number of hours available to me on any given day.

Multitasking, however, was not my major concern at that point; my monumental challenge was a massive migraine headache that came fully equipped with sensitivity to light and sound, mega-waves of nausea, blurred vision, and the inability to focus on even a single issue for any appreciable length of time.

And at that moment, the single issue was whatever rebuttal the opposing counsel had just presented in their opening statement that might refute our allegations of guilt against their client.

I tried to listen intently, but my mind had already drifted away from the current courtroom scene and was randomly racing through the next ten things on my agenda for that day; then backward to recapture segments of the disastrous (marital) mediation session from a few nights before, and then on to revisit the last conference I'd had with my daughter's principal regarding her in-school suspension because of her belligerent behavior.

Then there were those seemingly random images and snatches of conversations that I was trying to determine whether or not actually happened; or if they were premonitions of some future event; or were they just some convoluted craziness that my mind had conjured up as a result of the medication I had taken for my migraine the night before. Since I wasn't buying into the premonition theory, and I couldn't recall any solid evidence to substantiate them being actual memories...

AND, since all of the people involved in my recollections had appeared to be a menagerie of psychedelic colors, I was leaning strongly toward all of it being linked to the medication; so, I jotted down a note to call my doctor about switching that drug.

Although I was often plagued with headaches, they only intensified to this magnitude when I was under extreme stress, and since none of the previous ones had appeared in living color, this one was by far the worse I could ever recall. But then I'd say the stress load I was carrying at that time definitely qualified it for the mother of all migraines.

Taking into account the perpetual number of cases that continued to mound on my desk, the contentious attitude of my estranged (soon to be ex) husband after his adulterous affair, and add to that, more than a few calamitous mediation sessions, and the escalating escapades and misadventures of our teenage daughter; not to mention the ongoing scheming and conniving on constant rotation in the office... it was nothing short of a miracle that I had not shown up that day barefooted, wearing dark sunglasses, with a hoodie jacket atop my plaid PJs... blubbering some nonsensical rhetoric that no one, including me, could decipher.

Or even worse, what if I had simply not shown up at all? Had I opted for the latter, I may have been spared the embarrassment that followed during my 'zoned-out, lost in space' blackout.

The next thing I recall, I was being partially drawn back into the courtroom when I felt a tap on my hand and heard Elliott whisper something incoherent in my ear.

It wasn't until he raised his voice slightly and repeated his questions that I comprehended what he was saying. "Danielle, what's wrong? Are you okay? Do you need me to take over?"

Before I could respond, my eyes focused and locked in on the judge's inquisitive stare. I saw his lips moving, but initially heard no sound. After what felt like an eternity, I heard the sound of irritation booming in his voice, "For the third and final time - ADA Benson, I said, is the State ready to proceed?"

I could clearly hear and understand the question (that had apparently already been repeated twice), and I opened my mouth to answer, but was still caught up in a seemingly alternate dimension where everything appeared to be moving in extreme slow motion. My eyes moved around the courtroom from the Judge, to the bailiff, to Elliott, then to the defense attorneys and the defendant... to the members of the jury, and then the others present.

Everyone seemed to have this hazy glow about them, all in a rainbow of colors, and I was struggling desperately to try and determine what was happening. I remembered thinking, Okay Danielle, pull it together girl; it's just a reaction from those crazy drugs.

The last thing I remember was attempting to stand and speak, but instantly I felt another huge wave of nausea and lightheadedness, and then I felt myself slipping into the abyss of darkness.

THE COLOR OF CHARACTER

When my eyes opened, I was stretched out on the sofa in the judge's chamber with my suit jacket covering my legs. A clerk was sitting in the chair adjacent to the sofa, and a bailiff was standing between the sofa and the door. As I attempted to sit upright, the bailiff gently held my shoulder and said, "Just try to relax and lie still. The paramedics are on the way."

Paramedics?

Why were the paramedics coming? What happened? How did I get in here? As I fell gently back onto the sofa, I felt the blood rush to my head and I began to vaguely recall some of the events that had led up to the point where I apparently lost consciousness.

"Yes, please just lie still," the clerk echoed with a look of genuine concern. "Would you like a sip of water?"

I still had a putrid taste in my mouth, and just the thought of ingesting anything caused another tidal wave of nausea; so I kindly whispered "No thank you." I closed my eyes and tried to remain quiet and still, hoping the nausea would pass. I certainly did not want to create cause for any further alarm.

Shortly thereafter, the paramedics arrived, and I was loaded onto a stretcher and whisked off to the Emergency Room.

III

Not on My Agenda

The more I thought about the unplanned, unforeseen disruption to my day, the more I was convinced that what I was experiencing was some weird reaction to the medication that my doctor had prescribed; and although I was not at all pleased that I had to be carted off to the hospital in an ambulance, since I had to go, I was anxious to confer with the emergency room physician to see if they were in agreement with my suspicions regarding the medication.

I wasn't as concerned with being proven right, as I wanted to be assured that whatever the diagnosis, the cause of this episode could be cured, or at least corrected, so that I could get back to business as usual. My life was chaotic enough without this added complication.

"Hello Mrs. Benson, my name is Dr. Wallace. Can you tell me what brings you into the emergency room today?"

After recounting what I could, including my thoughts regarding the medication, I was relieved to hear the doctor agree that my suspicion could very well be a plausible reason for what was happening to me. He smiled and said, "Well it sounds like you've had quite a harrowing morning, but I think your suspicions about that medication could be correct.

Some of the drugs used to treat migraines are really potent and can sometimes cause some strange side effects. I suspect that your situation may be a combination of that, and some magnified symptoms of the headache itself. I'd like to order some tests, give you something to relieve your symptoms, and see how you're doing in a while."

Once he finished his exam, he left, and the nurse went about her tasks of drawing blood, entering things into the computer, and giving several medications through the IV.

ELAINE ROUNDTREE MONTFORD

"I'm giving you two different medicines for the nausea and vomiting, one for the pain and discomfort, and one specifically to relieve the migraine headache. These will cause you to be drowsy, so please do not attempt to get out of bed without assistance. I've put the orders in for the other tests Dr. Wallace mentioned, so someone will most likely be coming to get you in the next few minutes.

Meanwhile, would you like for me to turn your light out?"

In the time that it took me to nod *yes*, and for her to switch the light off and exit the room, I was already starting to feel the sedating effects of the medications. I closed my eyes and surrendered to the medicated induced slumber.

I was aroused from my slumber by the sound of someone calling my name. I opened my eyes to see a young man who announced that he was there to take me for x-rays.

Within just a few minutes, the x-ray study was completed and I was returned to my room. Upon my return, I found my husband Michael waiting. "Hi Danni, I got a call from your office saying you'd fallen ill in court and was brought here by ambulance. I tried calling your cell, but there was no answer, so I left a voicemail saying I would be here as soon as I could pick Justice up from school. How are you feeling?"

THE COLOR OF CHARACTER

"I'm feeling much better than earlier. I took some new medicine last night for my migraine, and it did a number on me! They've given me several medications since I've been here to counteract that, and I feel a marked improvement already. Between the episode itself, and the medicine they've given me here, I've been sort of out of it most of the day. I guess my phone is buried somewhere at the bottom of my purse, and most likely still on silent mode. Is Justice okay?"

Michael assured me that our daughter was fine and that of course, she wanted to come with him, but he thought it best to take her home since she tends to become quite nervous in this type of setting.

He told her he would call her as soon as he knew something regarding my condition.

In spite of the problems Michael and I were having, he was a wonderful father (even though he was not the biological father), and we did an exceptional job of co-parenting. It was sadly strange to me that I had not once thought about him, or even expected him to show up while I was there. I guess that was a pretty good indication of how tumultuous our marriage had become lately; and how far apart we had drifted.

It was as if he could interpret the sadness in my eyes, because just as I was entertaining that thought, he approached my bed, took my hand and said, "Contrary to what you may think or feel Danielle, I do still love you."

It had been such a long time since I had heard him utter those words, or speak to me so tenderly; and that reassurance felt good.

Somehow, I knew he was sincere…

Just as he leaned in to kiss me, Dr. Wallace returned with my test results.

"How are you feeling now, Mrs. Benson? Did that medication offer you any relief?"

"Yes, thank you, it was a tremendous help."

"Excellent! Well, I have the results of most of your tests; and I also took the liberty of speaking with Dr. Evans, your primary care physician. Most of your tests were completely normal, but there were a few slight abnormalities that are very likely your body's response to the trauma that this migraine has caused."

He chuckled lightly as he said, "Most migraines are the gift that keeps on giving."

Michael and I both smiled and nodded. "I do not believe that it's anything to be overly alarmed about; however, Dr. Evans and I both feel it would be beneficial to keep you for observation for about 24 hours or so, to see if we can continue to manage the pain and repeat some labs to determine if the pain management will reduce those elevated numbers."

I was even less thrilled with having to be admitted to the hospital than I was coming in the first place; but I was definitely feeling some relief, and I was a bit nervous about the abnormal test results. And even though my symptoms were improving, I was still seeing those halos of colors. Oddly enough, I was beginning to notice that it was only with certain individuals now.

Michael and Dr. Wallace both seemed to be sporting a soft white glow; while one of the nurses was sort of chartreuse green and the x-ray gentleman was a cross between blue and gray.

"Dr. Wallace, when will this colored halo effect cease?"

"I'm afraid I cannot give you an absolute on that one, but let's continue our course of treatment and see if it will take care of that issue. If it persists, we may have to refer you to a Neurologist for further evaluation."

Once Dr. Wallace had my consent for admission, he left to call Dr. Evans and inform him of my decision, and to give the E.R. nurse the thumbs up to secure a room for me on one of the observation floors.

I was giggling inside as I thought to myself, *well at least he said a neurological consult and not a psychological referral.*

IV

Learning From the Past

✵

Michael called Justice to bring her up to speed regarding the diagnosis and admission, and to ask if she needed him to pick up dinner for them, since he had volunteered to stay overnight with her at the house.

After fishing my phone from the bottom of my purse for me, and realizing the enormous number of missed calls and text messages; and after recognizing that there was very little life left on its battery, Michael readily offered me the use of his phone... but even more considerate of him, he graciously offered to respond to all of the inquiries himself so that I could continue to rest.

Without hesitation, I gratefully accepted the latter.

His loving gesture was quite reminiscent of the kind of consistent care that he would lavishly shower on me prior to the recent, somewhat rapid decline in our relationship, and the subsequent separation immediately thereafter. In fact, it was such a familiar scene, I began to consider in that moment whether what we had both viewed only a week or so earlier as irreconcilable differences, may have been a hasty decision based on vision that was clouded by pain, fueled by emotion, and motivated by an unwillingness on either of our parts to be proven wrong.

Michael and I were both strong-willed and passionate type "A" personalities, and when working together, we were pretty much an unstoppable force; but on the rare occasions when we found ourselves on opposing sides with no compromise in sight, the results were usually disastrous – unless one of us consented to concede.

I was seriously beginning to think that this might be the case with our relational woes and impending divorce. If this were indeed so, was I willing to lose another love of my life, and permanently disrupt our family simply because I was too proud to admit I may have been wrong?

My mind quickly flashed back to the break-up between Justice's biological father Jeremy, and me. Jeremy was my college love - I loved him with all of my heart, and I knew that he loved me equally, if not more. In fact, I would credit him with revealing to me what true love looked and felt like.

Before I met him, I had been given many examples of 'pseudo' love… selfishness and self-serving deception that was presented under the guise of "Love." Because that was all I had ever known, that was what I learned to reciprocate. Unlike me, Jeremy had grown up in a home environment where both parents were not only present, but participatory in his growth.

Jeremy would say that his parents were not afraid to display healthy love and affection for each other in the presence of himself and others, nor were they shy about showering it upon him.

He helped me to recognize that I was worthy of giving and receiving genuine love. I adored him; he was akin to a demi-god in my eyes. As far as I was concerned, he could do absolutely no wrong.

So, I was devastated when I suspected him of being unfaithful. The timing of this alleged impropriety was critical because it was shortly after I found out I was pregnant.

Everything in my life at that point took a paradigm shift. I became filled with pain and anger, and I lashed out at the one who I felt was responsible for causing it.

In actuality, I was petrified. I had fought and clawed my way through life and had finally reached a place where I felt I could be proud of my achievements; I had found the love of my life, was pregnant with our love child, and I was about to graduate with a law degree.

Life was good!

Then late one night, I spotted him sneaking out of another girl's dorm room - and BAM – I felt like life had sucker-punched me yet again.

He tried to explain why he was there, but I refused to listen. In a fit of rage, I announced my pregnancy and my disdain for him all in the same breath, and then abruptly stormed away. He tried on countless occasions after that night, to explain that he was not unfaithful, and he asked for the opportunity to prove his love for me and our child, but I allowed pride and un-forgiveness to shatter any hope of us ever being reconciled.

Jeremy even sought Samantha's help to plead his case, but her intercession fell on deaf ears as well. Sam made it clear to me that she believed Jeremy's explanation, and that she thought I had been overreacting; but she remained loving and supportive of me, despite my decision.

I was unaware (until recently) that Sam and Jeremy had stayed in contact over all those years. He would contact her on occasion to inquire about Justice, but apparently never failed to ask about me as well.

Ultimately, I had allowed my deep-seated fears and insecurities to rob me of a possible fairytale ending to a beautiful love story.

Michael came into our lives a couple of years later. He was such a refreshing breath of air after several unsuccessful attempts in the relationship department.

He was smart, and funny, and handsome, and passionate about the things he believed in. He was loving and giving, and strong... and imperfect. I was drawn to all of these qualities; but I think I was especially drawn to his imperfections because it allowed me to be myself without feeling I had to measure up to some unrealistic, self-imposed expectation that in order to deserve someone of this caliber, I had to be perfect.

What Jeremy had taught me about love, Michael taught me about acceptance, forgiveness, and grace. He proposed after six months of dating, and we married six months later.

Because Justice was so young when Michael and I met, and because she has never met her biological father, Michael became the only father she has ever known. Michael and I decided that when she was older, we would share the information about Jeremy with her because we both believe she deserves to know.

I looked up when I heard voices entering the room. Michael and the nurse were talking as they followed the young lady in who had come to transport me upstairs. Unlike the past few months, rather than cringe with contempt, my whole being lit up when I heard Michael's voice and saw his smiling face.

It was as if an ember had just been rekindled.

Could this be the beginning of a reconciliation? Is this what was needed to refocus our thoughts on each other rather than on our own selves, or our careers, or something or someone else?

I wasn't certain; but what I was sure of, was that I was at least willing to give it more thought, before I made my final decision in regard to the dissolution of our marriage.

V

Making Sense of the Nonsense
(The Shadow Walker)

Michael expressed his *thank you* to the Emergency room nurse as she disconnected me from the monitor and did a once over scan of the area to make sure that my clothes and any other personal items I had arrived with, went with us.

My attention, however, was captured by the soft glow of light around her that seemed to slightly obscure the rainbow of colors beneath it. The intensity of her light muted the kaleidoscope of swirling colors that blended into each other, continually creating a totally new pallet of colors. Her representation of colors was uniquely different from any other I had seen.

While everyone else's colors seemed to be separate and stagnant, hers seemed to have a life of their own; they were moving and changing with her every movement, with her every word, with her every thought. Her light seemed to respond to the changing colors – or were the colors changing in response to the light? I couldn't tell which one was the initiator of change... the colors or the light, but I knew they were intricately connected.

I also noticed that her light emitted a warmth that I could feel each time she was in close proximity to me. Now that I think about it, so did Michael and Dr. Wallace's.

Was this light the thing that had put me so at ease in their presence? Was this light the thing that had rekindled a spark between me and Michael? Was it the light or was it the colors?

Was I responding to both?

What I realized at that moment was that although I was still confused and fearful in regard to it all, my curiosity overrode my fear. I was intrigued by this new discovery.

My mind had begun to race a million miles a minute again; but unlike this morning's courtroom fiasco, it was not racing through random, unclear, disconnected thoughts. This time it was racing to connect clear, sharp thoughts and related incidents, in an effort to create a plausible theory.

But was I ready to accept this theory?

If this theory was correct, would it nullify my belief that visualization of these colors and light was simply a random, adverse reaction to some medication? And if it was due to the medication, was it safe to assume that once the medicine was gone, this phenomenon would also go away? What if it wasn't the medicine... what if it didn't go away?

What if it got worse?

Was I going crazy? Was I starting to lose touch with reality? What if I was truly one or two french-fries short of a happy meal?

Or, what if I had some sort of brain tumor? Now, my mind began to spin in these racing thoughts, and the more it spun, the more absurd my thoughts became.

The odd thing is, this time I recognized when things started spinning out of control, and I was able to slow the spin.

THE COLOR OF CHARACTER

I took in a deep breath and held it in.

Then I started to slowly exhale; all the while, silently talking myself into a quieter, less frantic head space.

I opened my eyes when the transporter announced that we had arrived at my room, and asked if I was able to walk a few steps from the stretcher to the bed.

Once I got settled into my room, the remainder of my night was fairly calm. Michael left, and my care team was in and out throughout the night checking my vital signs, administering medications, and drawing early morning bloodwork.

I vaguely remember segments of dreams throughout the night, but nothing that stood out or left a lasting impression. There were still the random images and fragmented conversations that appeared disjointed and without any significant connection. I also remembered seeing lights and colors of certain staff members that varied in intensity and hues; some stagnant and some more animated, but all still a mystery.

What I do distinctly remember, however, was one nursing aide who answered my call light when I needed assistance in the middle of the night.

ELAINE ROUNDTREE MONTFORD

Her color pallet was a swirling cauldron of various shades of gray, mahogany browns, indigo blues and deep crimson with intermittent black shadows. Her presence brought an unsettling coldness despite the smile and calmness she attempted to present.

I felt a bone shuttering chill as soon as she walked in. As she came closer, I noticed that there was an emptiness about her eyes that was hard to describe, but it was like peering into a black hole. They say that our eyes are *the window to the soul*, and if this is true, then I suspect that her soul had long since lost any hint of light.

In fact, I suspect that everything about her preferred darkness to light; hiding in the shadows, under the cover of darkness.

I was immediately uncomfortable and on guard from the very moment she came into my presence. Oddly enough, this was the first time since this strange phenomenon had begun that I was assured of what I was feeling, and I was completely confident that I'd felt this way a few times before. Something or someone very evil had just entered my room... and I did not need super powers or extreme psychic abilities to recognize it.

"Yes, my lady, how may I help you?"

My bladder was so full it felt like it would pop, but I could not imagine allowing her to assist me with anything, let alone leave her in my room out of my sight, while I was closed off in the bathroom. I had to think of something quickly to get her out of my room, and away from me. "Oh, I'm so sorry; I must have accidentally hit my call light."

"No problem, ma'am."

She stood there for a moment, her eyes boring holes through me, as if scrutinizing my response, or waiting for me to reconsider or resend it; then she abruptly turned and left. As soon as she was out of sight, although I was not supposed to get up without assistance, I scurried into the bathroom to relieve my bladder.

I remember thinking – Whoa! What was that?! What just happened? Where did she come from? I may not have been able to answer all those questions, but one thing was unequivocally clear... that was evil incarnate.

My analytical mind began to engage in the next level of connect-the-dots; but very few dots were connecting. I pondered how anyone could make sense of things that appeared to be completely illogical; those things that just do not compute in your head, but your inner sense tells you that something is terribly wrong. How does one "make sense out of nonsense?"

I didn't know, but I was desperately trying to do just that.

I tried to recollect my thoughts from my very first memory of questionably authentic conversations and images, to my visual perception of an individual's unique color rainbow, and then those panoramic scenes of events that played like a nostalgic motion picture in my mind's eye.

It was obvious that I was the only one seeing and hearing things in this manner; but what did it all mean? Where did it come from, and what was I supposed to do with this information, be it real or imagined?

Unnerved by that encounter with the aide from the dark side, I wasn't comfortable with the idea of going to sleep, so I switched on the TV and waited for daybreak.

VI

As Different as Night and Day

✹

As the morning rolled in, it was as if a giant had been awakened; there was an increased level of activity in the hallway as the staff changed shifts.

As hard as I had tried to stay awake, I realized that I must have drifted back to sleep, because I was aroused from my slumber by voices outside my door and the pleasant sound of gentle humming, and an intense light that I initially assumed was merely the sunlight peeking through the window in my room.

My eyes opened to spot an elderly lady with silver hair and glowing brown skin, slightly plump in size, and an amazingly beautiful smile; she was mopping the floor over near the window.

"Good morning Ma, this just Miss Clara doing a little housekeeping; I pray I didn't disturb you," she chirped in her rhythmic islander dialect.

"Good morning; no, you didn't disturb me at all."

As she moved away from the window and about the room, I noticed that the greater majority of light moved with her.

She was like a glowing prism of energized light and color, each independent of the other, yet all blending and fusing in one fluid motion. "You are like the sunshine... but the residue of the dark one still lingers here, and it is giving me soul a chill," she said as she smiled brightly. Then her smile abruptly dimmed and her body shuttered, while her eyes surveyed the room, in an attempt to locate the source of her discomfort.

It was as if I not only heard her words, but literally felt them. My entire being felt the warmth of the sun when she spoke of it, and I felt a deep chill when she spoke of the dark one.

Although she appeared to be 15-20 years my senior, she moved with the focus and energy of someone half my age - it was like looking at my mother, with my daughter's level of energy. She seemed to float across the floor, and her mop appeared to flow in perfect synchronization with her... a familiar partner in a well-rehearsed dance.

She seemed to know all of the unanswered questions that lingered in my mind, and her light illumined the portion of my soul where all of those answers were waiting to be unlocked.

It felt as if time stood still, or was moving in slow motion again, but unlike the courtroom debacle, this time there was no angst, no confusion, and no illness. This time there was pure peace and clarity; a wholeness such as I had never experienced before. I totally surrendered all of me to that moment, and it was in that moment I began to discover a part of me that I never knew existed.

Her presence had ignited a light within me, and suddenly the murky, cloudy waters of unexplainable incidents were beginning to become just a bit clearer. In the short time she was in my presence that morning, I received more clarity than I had in months.

...Maybe even years.

"Take heed to what I say. God, He gives each of us someteng... but He never gives anyone everyteng. Udderwise, dat one wit it all, his pride swell greater than de sea; den he begin to tink he da god! Yes, Honey, de good Lord give each of us someteng special, and we can either see it as a gift or a curse. But if we use de gift, it will guide us through de darkness. Dis ole world be full of colors – some bright and some dark, and de people dey wear deir character like Joseph's coat. Some of dem walk in de light, and some dey lurk in da shadows. Da shadow walkers, dey say in deir heart, 'You dun see me mon'; but me heart sees dem all – de good, and de bad; de Light dwellers and de shadow walkers."

She let out a hearty chuckle that filled the room like waves of the ocean, and for that instant, I knew what pure joy felt like - and for the first time in a very long time, my heart smiled.

It was as if her every word carried with it new life; and I was the fortunate recipient of this soul-stirring revival.

THE COLOR OF CHARACTER

It was an interesting dichotomy, because I had never felt so energized, so rejuvenated; yet my entire being was totally relaxed and at peace.

She finished her impromptu sermon with, "But dees eyes o mine, dey see ya gift in de light, and ya soul, it has great insight... so don't let ya head discount what ya heart can see. Trust ya gift dawta, and it will lead you safely home."

I was amazed at how she had answered questions I had entertained, but not yet spoken; and how she had so freely exposed the secret that had haunted me ever since this phenomenon had manifested. And, I was sincerely grateful for the revelation that I was not the only one with this ability.

Who was this mysterious little lady and where had she come from? How did she know about my encounter with that dark spirit a few hours prior? How did she know about the colors? More importantly, why did she in no way feel like a stranger to me, nor I to her? She was more like the answer to a prayer, and I was ready to bear my soul to her as if she was a trusted confidant.

All of these questions raced from my head to my heart like flaming arrows fired from a skilled archer's bow.

I sat in utter amazement at her insight and wisdom. Everything about her intrigued me; and I was content to sit at her feet and learn, for as long as she was willing to share.

She continued to hum and waltz her way around the room until her task was complete, and then she placed her mop back in the pail. And just like that, she smiled and made her exit as quietly as she had entered.

This was the second time in less than 24 hours that I was confident of what I had experienced. The first entity was pure evil incarnate, but this one was pure, unadulterated life energy that was enveloped by Light, and wrapped in a layer of beautiful brown flesh.

I was equally sure that both had been in existence since the beginning of time in one form or another; and I knew that I would encounter them both again.

VII

Embracing the Gift

✷

I felt such a sense of relief after my encounter with Miss Clara; she had somehow validated my sanity, and restored my peace. In fact, everything about me seemed to have been enhanced. After weeks and months of wrestling with confusion and uncertainty, I finally had a keen sense of clarity.

Now I needed to seriously consider how to navigate this new territory. Even though I was fascinated by Miss Clara's revelatory information, I was also still extremely cautious in regard to both *who* and *how* I would share this delicate information.

Who could I turn to for guidance? Were there others like me, and if so, how and where would I find them?

I made a mental list of family and friends, and began to cross off the ones I knew for sure were completely out of the question. When I surveyed my list, I had quickly eliminated all, but two; and one of them was suspect. I tried to imagine how I would respond if I had never experienced any of this, and someone attempted to share their experiences with me. I laughed because I would have been one of the first who would have been eliminated from the "trusted to tell list."

Not because I'm untrustworthy, but because I would have questioned the authenticity of the information.

Realizing that I was having a challenge just trying to come up with someone I could share this with, I strongly considered not telling anyone at all, and attempting to go on with life as if none of this existed.

Unfortunately, that was not a viable option for me because in my opinion, that would be tantamount to un-ringing a bell –I wouldn't be able to un-know, or ignore it.

But I could not imagine trying to deal with this issue any longer by myself; this was too heavy a weight to bear singly. As independent and capable as I was, I knew I was going to need some help with this one.

I decided the best place to start was with the "revelator" herself, Miss Clara. She obviously held a wealth of knowledge; so what better place to start. It was apparent from our initial meeting that she possessed the same gift, and that she operated at a much higher level, so perhaps she would be willing to teach me how to perfect my gift.

It was still early in the day, so I felt sure she was still on the clock. I hit the call button and waited for the nurse or aide to respond. When the aide responded, I asked if it was possible for me to speak with Miss Clara, the sweet lady from environmental service who had cleaned my room earlier.

The aide gave me a curious look, and asked me to repeat the worker's name... so again I repeated, "Miss Clara."

She said, "We had a Miss Clara who used to work on this floor for many years, but she passed away three years ago. Are you sure of the name?"

I said, "Yes, I'm certain she said Clara; she was an older brown-skinned lady with a beautiful smile, and a pronounced Island accent."

"Hmm, that is really strange, that sounds exactly like Miss Clara.... but it can't be; she's passed on."

I said, "Is there another Miss Clara, or someone who looks or sounds like her?"

"No, there's no one working on this floor in that department who even comes close."

We both looked at each other in disbelief.

After an awkward pause, the aide asked, "Did you need housekeeping; I can find someone for you."

I was still stunned, and I wasn't quite sure how to respond; so I just nodded my head and said "no thank you."

I had no clue what to do now. Miss Clara was the validator of my sanity and my gift; now she appeared to no longer be alive, let alone a legitimate witness.

EPILOGUE

That level of confidence and peace that I had experienced immediately following my encounter with Miss Clara was starting to fade; and I knew if I shared any of my supernatural experiences with anyone else, they would surely have me transferred to a psychiatric unit for the rest of my life.

Hopefully, the aide would chalk my inquiry of Miss Clara up to my medication, and not start spreading rumors among the staff about the 'crazy lady in room 212'.

The fact remained that I needed to tell someone about my experiences, and the only other person I trusted to that degree was in the number two slot on my *go tell* list. We had been to hell and back together; she would either support me as she always has... or she would personally deliver me to the nearest mental institution.

I picked up my cell phone and hit number two on the speed dial. *This is Samantha; I'm sorry I missed your call – please leave a brief message and I'll get back to you. Shalom.*

"Hey Sam, this is Danni... give me a call when you get this. I really need your ear. I love you... talk to you soon."

For the first time in the past few days, I began to see this phenomenon in a somewhat different light. I started to recognize that the very thing I had viewed as a serious flaw or defect just might be one of my greatest assets, because it gave me the ability to visualize a person's character in living, breathing color and light.

At that moment it was as if I could see into my soul; and there stood Miss Clara, flashing that beautiful smile. Immediately my peace returned, and that was all the validation I needed.

The Other Sister

And he said, a certain man had two sons:

And the younger of them said to his father, Father, give me the portion of goods that falleth to me.

And he divided unto them his living.

And not many days after the younger son gathered all together, and took his journey into a far country, and there wasted his substance with riotous living…

Now his elder son was in the field: and as he came and drew nigh to the house, he heard musick and dancing. And he called one of the servants, and asked what these things meant. And he said unto him, Thy brother is come; and thy father hath killed the fatted calf, because he hath received him safe and sound.

And he was angry, and would not go in: therefore came his father out, and intreated him. And he answering said to his father, Lo, these many years do I serve thee, neither transgressed I at any time thy commandment: and yet thou never gavest me a kid, that I might make merry with my friends. But as soon as this thy son was come, which hath devoured thy living with harlots, thou hast killed for him the fatted calf.

And he said unto him, Son, thou art ever with me, and all that I have is thine.

It was meet that we should make merry, and be glad: for this thy brother was dead, and is alive again; and was lost, and is found.

~Luke 15:11-13;25-32

"But, it's *my* money!"

"You're right, in a way. It's in your name..."

"Then, I don't see why you won't give it to me! You know I need it now!"

"Derán, you will get it. But, it's in a Trust until you're 21."

"That's six months from now! What am I going to do until then?!"

Synithia sighed deeply and tried to concentrate on the manuscript she was currently editing. She had been increasingly losing focus for the past hour, as the argument between her father and sister continued to escalate; not only in volume, but also in intensity. Her headphones were no longer providing the insulated oasis they had for the previous half hour and if she turned the sound up any higher, she risked damaging her ears.

It was time to invest in a noise-cancelling headset.

"Dad, you just don't understand. My rent is late, my car needs the air conditioner replaced, and my student loan repayment begins in a few months. And, I have things I want to do... places I want to go. I'm sick of hanging around here. It's boring and we never do anything. I hate the people here and they hate me."

Not waiting to listen to her father's paternally gentle response to Derán's continuing tirade, Synithia went ahead and increased the sound level on her music, and clicked 'OK' on the warning that popped up on her newly acquired Samsung Galaxy Note that said:

> **"Listening at a high volume for
> a long time may damage your hearing.
> Tap OK to allow the volume
> to be increased above safe levels."**

She had work to do and the distraction was only going to cause her to miss the project deadline.

This back and forth between her father and younger sister had been going on for almost a year now; ever since their mother had passed, following a long and debilitating illness. The loss of her mom was a painful memory, so Synithia quickly shrugged the thought aside and forced herself to stay focused on the words in front her.

So, while the sound of her favorite song repeated again and again, Synithia became intent on perfecting the writing in the Word document on the computer monitor, and allowed herself to get completely lost both in the task at hand and in the heavy beat that pounded in her ears.

The soft touch on the back of her shoulder almost sent her scrambling head-first over the top of her desk.

"Oh, Dee Dee! You scared me spitless!"

"Girl please..." Derán retorted, falling heavily onto Synithia's freshly made, King-sized platform bed. "I knocked on your door for almost a minute and called your name five times. Whatchu working on?"

"I'm doing a substantive edit on one of my client's drafts; getting it ready for release by the end of this month."

"Mmmm... you've been in here for a long time," Derán said, lying on her back and looking up at the ceiling. "You really need to get out more. Since Mommy died, all you do is sit at this desk and work. You're no fun anymore."

THE OTHER SISTER

"What else do you want me to do? Spend my days arguing with Daddy about the insurance money, like you?"

The silence was instantly palpable and Synithia could immediately feel the hurt and pain that flashed across her younger sister's face, as if she had stabbed her in the heart with a dull knife.

"Well, Mommy left that money for us and I need it," Derán retorted, a bit more like an upset five-year-old who wasn't being given the handful of cookies she wanted to eat before dinner, than the mature young lady she actually was. "I don't know why she left Daddy in charge of it; it's like he's getting a kick out of making life miserable for me... almost as if it makes him happy to see me so unhappy!"

Synithia gently smiled and, much like her father, found herself trying to reason with Derán. "Dee Dee, now I know you're aware of the proviso Mom included in the Will, just like I am. She required an 18-month holding period before funds could be dispersed and that you were also over 21. She wanted to make sure that we had money for the future and didn't blow it all two seconds after we got it."

"Blah blah blah... *yada yada yada*. It also said that Daddy had discretion to give it to us earlier if there was a hardship or issue, and I need mines now Sissy," Derán replied as she sat up on the edge of the bed.

Suddenly, with a surprisingly excited look crossing her face, she swung her feet onto the floor and stood up. "What if we both went to him and asked for it? If you told him you needed your money too, then I know he would go ahead and release it. He can't say *no* to both of us, right?"

Synithia slowly nodded her head. Truth be told, she could use an influx of cash right now. Contract payables had been coming in slow, and she needed to upgrade her equipment, resources, and tools if she were to implement some of the project deliverables she had planned for the firm's upcoming quarter.

Taking a deep breath, Synithia simply said, "Okay."

Squealing, Derán grabbed her by the arm and almost pulled her and the office chair she was sitting in onto the floor.

"Hold on! Hold on! Let me at least finish this edit and get it back to the client. We'll talk to him after dinner, alright?"

THE OTHER SISTER

"Okie Dokie," her sister squeaked, skipping to the door. "Let's do this!"

"Shut the door, please!" Synithia yelled before returning her attention to the monitor and placing the headset buds back into her ears, the music still playing on repeat; as she began making a mental list of all the things she could buy with her portion of the inheritance.

Wow! This place is really packed... I'm sure we will have a good time tonight!"

Synithia looked around the room. Her bestie, Monee was right. Atlanta nightlife was always poppin' on the weekends, but this club was so full, she was sure the Fire Marshall would be closing the place down long before last call. The DJ had a hot Old School rap mix playing so loudly, it was difficult to hold a real conversation; not to mention the flashing lights already threatening to give her a headache.

It had been two years since their Daddy had gone ahead and released the Trust funds to Synithia and Derán. Business was good and life was good. So, instead of complaining, she went ahead and handed over her credit card to secure bottle service for a VIP table package for Girls Night Out.

THE OTHER SISTER

The $1500 minimum gave the small group of ladies the ability to skip entry lines, while also keeping them from having to stand around like sardines in a can or squeeze into a few solitary seats along the exceptionally tight floor space.

As they were being escorted to a booth on the second level overlooking the huge dance floor, Michel, one of her sister-friends exclaimed, "Gurrl... there are some good-looking men in this spot, for sure!"

Amber, another one of her childhood friends, responded with equal exuberance. "You ain't ever lied. I know I'm not going home alone tonight."

The third, Crystal, couldn't help but add her commentary regarding the quality of men around them. "I know that's right. Me and that so-called thot of mine need a break from one another. And this is just the place to get it."

"Yeah", Michel said lyrically, mixing in a Mickey D's jingle to the tune and rhythm of the hip hop song currently blasting through the speakers. *"You deserve a break today!"*

Laughing, they sat down, and Synithia placed an order for a bottle of Gran Patrón Platinum, a bottle of Grey Goose, a bottle of Appleton Estate, and the standard complimentary mixers of cranberry juice, pineapple juice, tonic water, and Coca-Cola.

"This is a great table," Monee chirped. We can get a good view of all the men from here."

Hmmph... Synithia thought to herself, while the lifetime friends giggled and chatted among themselves.

Taking a second look around the room, she realized that she recognized a well-groomed dark skinned brother in a booth on the other side of the floor.

It was Marcus Smith... an old friend from High School.

Excusing herself, she made her way toward the visage of manhood she had discovered. She wanted to see if he still looked as delicious up close.

Yes... Why, yes, he does, she muttered as she reached handshake distance to him, and he stood to greet her.

Synithia looked up, and tried to take in all 6.2 inches of his strong, muscular build. Dressed in a navy, single-button Armani, her senses were intrigued.

He had grown since she last saw him.

After a short embrace, he invited her to join him. "Would you like to sit with us for a minute?" he asked, motioning to an empty seat at the booth he shared with one other person.

"Sure. Why not?" she answered, sliding in and scooting over, so that Marcus could come in behind her.

"What would you like to drink?"

"Can I get a Cuervo Gold on the rocks? No salt, please."

"You got it!" Marcus gave the order to the hostess and then proceeded to introduce her to his friend. "This is my boy Drake. Drake, this is Cynthia."

"Synithia"

"That's right, I'm sorry. Synithia. This is Synithia."

"It's okay. Nice to meet you, Drake."

Drake reached over and shook her hand, giving her a warm smile. "It's nice to meet you too."

Maintaining a poker face after hearing the sound of his voice, which sounded like a warm baritone that rode right through the heavy bass lines in the music that continued to fill the club, Synithia returned her attention to the object of her initial intrigue.

"So, Marcus... It's been a while. What have you been up to all of these years?"

"Oh, me? Well, after school, I moved down to Florida to attend FAMU and get my degree in Philosophy and Religion."

"That sounds amazing. What are you doing now?"

"I pastor a small church in Fort Lauderdale. I'm up here now for a Leadership Conference this weekend and thought I'd drop in on my best friend before things got started. And, I'm glad I did."

Synithia was a little surprised, both to know that Marcus had chosen this career path and that as a man of God, he would be hanging out at a night spot, but quickly dismissed it.

He was chocolate goodness wrapped in a suit.

The rest of the evening went well; her girls had a wonderful time. Or, at least that's all Synithia cared enough to remember. While they drank up the minimum and acted like 'big baller-shot callers' on her dime, she spent the bulk of her evening in Marcus' presence. Even those few times she went back to check on them, the two of them kept each other within line of sight.

Just shy of midnight, she signed the credit card slip and told the crew they were on their own.

She had grown woman plans for the rest of the night.

Marcus and Synithia drove to the northwestern edge of Midtown, parked the car in the underground garage at Atlantic Station, and walked the stairs to the street; walking and talking their way down 17th Street.

Once they arrived at the room he was staying in at the Twelve Hotel, he opened the door and let her in first.

She was ready.

Slowly undressing, she stepped out of her Louboutin's and began removing the small string of pearls from around her neck.

Following her lead, Marcus picked Synithia up in his arms and carried her into the bedroom; setting her down in front of the bed. Pulling him onto it, Synithia jumped on top of him and began kissing him on his neck.

Softly, she asked, "Are *you* ready?"

Marcus waited with bated breath as the number he had just dialed rang once, then twice, then a third time. He glanced at the number on the yellow sticky note that he held in his hand one more time; making sure that he had dialed it correctly, and then continued to wait as the line rang a fourth time.

Just as he began to think that Synithia was not available and he would be sent to voicemail, there was a knock on the hotel room door.

He disconnected the call.

"Happy Monday Pastor," Synithia said cheerfully.

"Happy Monday. How are you this morning?" Marcus responded, not quite sure how this encounter was going to go; especially since they hadn't had a chance to speak since Saturday morning. Although he had thoroughly enjoyed the time spent together Friday night, he had begun feeling a bit convicted.

But, good lord was she looking extremely lovely this morning! Dressed in an all-white, cotton knit Ralph Lauren dress that stopped midway between the thigh and knee and hugging every voluptuous curve she had, Synithia entered the room and walked right past Marcus, to take a seat on the small sofa; forcing him to take the scenic route with his eyes in order to view her from the top of her legs, beyond her waist, and eventually to her behind.

He couldn't help but smile.

"My morning just got better, Sir. How are you doing?" she asked, as he sat down next to her and gently kissed her on the forehead, allowing the masculine fragrance of his Giorgio Armani's *Acqua Di Gio* to mesh ever so sweetly with her Thierry Mugler's *Angel*; the perfect blend of earthly male and female energies.

Marcus shook his head and the small amount of resolve he had to do right was quickly ebbing away. "It is well Synithia... it is well." Changing the subject, he shared with her that he had just tried to call her.

"...and here I am!" Synithia replied, with a sly grin. "Great minds truly do think alike."

Trying to find something else, anything else, to focus on, Marcus began to rearrange items on the hotel room desk.

"Hey. Tell me more about your friend, Drake. How do you guys know each other?" Synithia asked.

"He's one of my best friends," Marcus answered. "He's a law student over at Howard."

Synithia's attention was instantly piqued. "Law student? How did you two become friends?"

"We met through some mutual friends here in the A. We used to play basketball together. You saw him Synithia. You know I'm tall, but Drake stands almost a full head taller than me!"

"Yes, he is seriously one tall drink of water!" Synithia said, unconsciously looking up.

Marcus didn't know why, but he wasn't sure if he was more unnerved by Synithia's comment or the fact that she was here at all. What was it that was making him experience such a mixture of emotions? Why was he feeling a sense of dread and excitement at the same time?

"It's too early in the morning for all of this," Marcus inadvertently said out loud.

"Too early for what? All, I'm saying is that he must be tall," Synithia retorted, backing up defensively.

Marcus groaned. "No... uh. I'm sorry. I didn't mean anything by it. I was just thinking about all the things I need to get done today." He bowed his head a bit and gave her his best 'puppy dog eyes', hoping that she would come stand close enough to him again to have the sweet aroma of her perfume back in his nostrils.

Synithia giggled and obliged him by sitting on his lap. "How about we grab some breakfast before you leave?" she whispered in his good ear.

"Mmm... I could eat," Marcus responded, teasingly.

"Excellent. Breakfast it is, Pastor Smith," Synithia said as she slowly lifted herself off of his legs and provocatively walked back toward the door.

Marcus momentarily forgot about his travel plans for the day as he allowed his senses to linger a few moments longer in the cloud of perfume left by Synithia's departure from the couch. "God help me," he said to no one in particular.

The short thirty five minute drive home North to Suwanee from Midtown, seemed like floating on air. And, it wasn't just the obviously smooth ride of her Mercedes C500 that made it so.

The seemingly coincidental reintroduction to Marcus felt God-ordained; divinely arranged.

Here was a man who was much like her... educated, intelligent, purposed, and gorgeous. They were alike in so many ways and fit together perfectly. This was it!

And, he was a man of God.

After all of the busters and scrubs she had been encountering over the past couple of years, she was ready for someone real; someone who would be loving and faithful to her. Someone who could partner with her in life and make something amazing happen.

It was time…

Synithia tuned the satellite radio station to a gospel channel and the inspirational music flowing through the Benz's Bose speakers helped to support her relaxed and calm spirit.

Her mobile phone rang through the system.

"Hello?"

"Hey Synithia."

She recognized his voice immediately. "Missing me already, huh?" she said teasingly.

"Yeah… listen. I need to say something and I need you to hear me. Okay?"

"Sure. What's going on?"

"I… I can't do this, Synithia," Marcus said.

"Can't do what?"

After a short pause, he continued. "I can't be in a relationship with you. This isn't right. I'm not right."

"What the… Are you serious right now?!"

"I'm so sorry, Synithia. I really like you and I enjoyed being with you, but…" Struggling to find the words, Marcus hesitated and then simply said, "Please forgive me," before hanging up the phone.

The melodious voice of CeCe Winans' singing the second verse of *Alabaster Box* began to take up space in the stunned atmosphere that swiftly filled the car's cabin.

Synithia turned off the radio and rode the rest of the way home in silence.

THE OTHER SISTER

When Synithia turned the corner onto the street where she and her father lived, her daddy's Range Rover could be seen in the driveway. This was unusual, because it was the middle of the day and he would normally be at the office.

Pulling into the drive, Synithia hit the garage door opener, and slowly brought the Benz around the SUV, being very careful not to come too close to it. Thankfully, the driveway was built wide enough that even though her father had parked off center, rather than closer to the right edge, she was able to easily maneuver herself into the two and a half car garage from the far left side, without any issues.

Once Synithia walked into the house, to find her father at the kitchen table with his cellphone in his hand, she quickly went on alert; not quite sure what to expect.

However, she was met with an enormous grin and a spirit of joy radiating from his being.

It literally filled the room.

"What's going on, Daddy?"

"You'll never believe it Baby. Your sister sent me a text earlier this morning. She's coming home!"

Synithia set her purse and car keys on the kitchen counter and then sat down in one of the chairs on the opposite side of her father.

"Dee Dee's coming home? When?"

"This weekend," her father answered, scanning a list of names and phone numbers written on the piece of paper lying on the table in front of him. "I've been calling all of the friends on your and Derán's contact list all morning to invite everyone to a welcome home party this Saturday!"

"A party! Why?"

"Why not? Your Sister has been gone for the past two years and we've heard nothing from her all this time and now she is coming home. Aren't you excited to see her?"

Synithia could feel the anger slowly rising from the pit of her stomach, as it made its way through her chest cavity into the back of her throat. It took all she had to keep the taste of burning bile from spilling into her mouth.

"Daddy! Of course, I'm excited to see Derán. But, why would you have a party for her? She begged and begged you for that money and then as soon as you gave it to her, she left us!"

"Right, but I gave you your money too, Synithia..."

"And I stayed here!" Synithia said, her voice getting louder. "I stayed here with you. Yet, in all this time, you've never even considered having a party for me! Now that your precious babygirl, who has thrown away all of the money you and Mommy set aside for her comes home, you want to turn up for her!"

Pushing his chair back, Synithia's father leaned back and looked lovingly at his eldest daughter. "Yes Sissy, you stayed with me. And that means that you not only received your portion of the funds to spend as you pleased, but you also continued to have access to everything I have.

Not just material things, like that car you're driving and the clothes you get to wear, but also the creature comforts you enjoy, like hot water and air conditioning... a safe and secure place to lay your head each night, or as much food as you want to eat. You also had the opportunity to receive the daily benefit of my love and grace. So, you lacked nothing Synithia, because you had me with you... always."

The anger that had just moments before threatened to spew onto the dark marble table between her and her father quickly ebbed into a dull heartache; with its only evidence being a single tear slowly sliding down the side of her cheek.

"Do you not see how much I love you?" her father continued. "Do you not know how precious you are to me? That I don't judge you for your behavior? That I am fully aware of what you are you doing late at night and over the weekends?" I don't say anything because you are an adult and you have to live with the consequences of your decisions.

And, so does your Sister."

Leaning in and laying his forearms onto the table, he folded his hands and spoke in the same paternally gentle voice he had used with Derán years earlier, "But neither of you will ever lose me. No matter what... I will always love you. I will never leave you, nor will I ever abandon you; especially when you need me most."

He paused... "and Derán needs me now."

THE OTHER SISTER

The tears were in full flow now, as if to flush away the residue of sadness which had remained following the loss of her mother, the resentment and bitterness that had built up since Derán had left, and the new pain of being used and then rejected by a man she had no business with in the first place.

Synithia now realized that the greater gift had been in her presence all along, and she had taken it for granted; treating it as common.

Getting up from her seat, she went to hug her father, feeling as if she couldn't get to him fast enough.

He met her before she got around the corner of the table; holding her tightly and letting her tears soak the front of his multi-breasted suit jacket.

"I'm sorry Daddy."

Drake Jones was deep in concentration.

Sitting in one of the assigned carrels at the Allan Mercer Daniel law library at Howard, reserved for first thing that Monday morning, Drake was intently poring over several cases needed to prepare for a class coming up later that afternoon.

Being a full-time third year law student was no joke. It took every amount of effort for him to be able to stay on top of things and not get behind in his studies. Drake had known for a very long time that he would have to work hard to get where he wanted to be in life, so the effort required was neither an inconvenience nor a surprise to him.

And, he was not one to make excuses to himself or make excuses for himself. Just because he had been raised by a single mother in an impoverished neighborhood didn't mean that he could just lie back and blame life for what he was or was not given. He had learned early in life not to sit around and wait for life to happen or to hand him what he needed, let alone wanted.

This was a totally different way of thinking from his three brothers and two sisters, though; or, should he say half brothers and sisters, since the only thing they shared in common was that they had the same mother. Drake didn't even know his own father.

Oh, he knew his father's name, where he lived, that his father was married and that he had another brother and sister with that same father; but, if his dad were to walk right up to him today in this library, he wouldn't even recognize him.

He had been told that he looked a lot like him. Not exactly like him, but a definite resemblance. He was a perfect blending and merging of both his mother and father; which apparently was a good thing since he was quite attractive.

The height? Direct from his father.

The entire time he had been growing up, he was constantly reminded by those who knew his father that he was exceptionally tall just like him. At 6 feet 7, it was a great icebreaker and garnered him much attention from males and females alike; for various reasons.

It was something Drake greatly enjoyed and it allowed him to carry himself with a high level of ease and confidence without having to work too hard at it. He knew that the moment he stood up or walked into a room, people were paying close attention to him. Now it was up to him to make sure that he also had a great mind to go with that great door opener.

And yes, all stereotypes aside, he was an awesome basketball player!

Being tall and good at ball was what had landed him the opportunity to get a college education at absolutely no cost to himself.

What they called *a full ride*.

But, Drake wanted to be acknowledged for being so much more than just another dumb jock. He wanted people to respect him for being mentally sharp as well; that when he opened his mouth, people listened because they recognized that he knew what he was talking about. And, he didn't want people to automatically know that he fit the stereotype perfectly; just a poor black boy from out of the projects, without benefit of expensive private schools, who had gotten out only because he could handle a ball well.

He was a heck of lot more than that!

The vibrating phone in his jacket pocket broke through his thoughts.

"unknown caller"

Instantly curious, Drake got up, hastily made his way out of the carrel, through the library, and toward the main door. Swiping his touchscreen to answer the call, he said, he answered the phone.

"This is Drake..."

Saturday afternoon was a whirlwind of activity, with final arrangements being made and last-minute changes being implemented. At the end of it all, the event hall was beautiful.

No, it was stunning!

Their father had spared no expense and every detail demonstrated nothing less than excellence. This was a party fashioned and designed for the daughter of a king.

Synithia hung the bag containing her sister's gown for the evening on the hook in the dressing room and unzipped it. As she prepared to take the red off-the-shoulder Chiara Boni La Petite Robe out of the garment bag, she caught a glimpse of herself in the wall-to-wall dressing mirror. Wearing a form-fitting black crepe back cutout by Vera Wang that she had purchased the day before at Nordstrom, she smiled.

THE OTHER SISTER

She felt pretty good about everything.

The soft knock on the open door pulled her out of her reverie. "Hey Sissy."

Turning, Synithia's eyes met her baby sister's and held them for almost a full minute before she could speak. This was not the same Derán who had left. A new woman had taken her place.

A stronger woman. A wiser woman.

The two sisters embraced and loved on one another; exclaiming how beautiful the other was.

"Girl, look at you... you are gorgeous!"

"What!? No... You are gorgeous! I'm gonna need work to catch up with you!"

"Pffft... whatchu talkin' bout? That dress is gon' kill 'em!"

"Check this..." Synithia pulled her sister's dress out and placed it in front of her body, like a cut-out paper doll.

"BAM!"

With a squeal reminiscent of the old Dee Dee, Derán grabbed the exquisite gown from Synithia and immediately began to change her outfit.

Giggling, Synithia left her sister to it, and exited the dressing room to begin greeting incoming guests. Shutting the door, she made her way down the back hall toward the dimly lit banquet room and sounds of Luther's *"A House is Not a Home."*

She saw him from across the room. He was standing by the hors d'oeuvres table; placing a few teaspoons of the roasted garlic aioli on the Mikasa crystal appetizer plate, alongside a small serving of the crudité.

He certainly cuts an attractive figure, Synithia thought to herself, as she took two flutes filled with champagne from the server nearest her, and approached him.

"Good evening. I'm so glad you could make it," she said, handing him one of the glasses.

Taking it in his free hand, he smiled. "Thank you for inviting me. You guys really did an amazing job... everything looks exceptional.

"You can credit my Daddy for all of this. Nothing is too good for his daughters."

"So, I see," he replied. "I am definitely taking notes."

"Nah. Just remember one thing," Synithia replied softly. Love is the most precious gift. Things will fail, money will fail, people will fail. But, it is a truth love never fails. So, if it fails, it wasn't love."

At that moment, Derán entered the room; the red gown flattering and accentuating her youthful figure.

Synithia discreetly motioned for her to come over.

Handing her the second champagne flute, she took her hand and said, "Drake, this is my sister Derán." Then, taking the plate from his hand, she said, "Dee Dee, this is Drake.

I hope you two have a wonderful time."

A Forbidden Love

Prologue

Remembering...

Amiha let out a very long and loud sigh, as she overheard, the doctors talking with her mother and family members. 'Has she ever done anything like this before?' Were there any signs leading to this?

In unison, they all responded, no, not at all.

The doctors looked at the family and surmised that they were speaking truth. "Well, the medicines that she ingested have been in her system too long to pump her stomach, doing so, will have little if no impact, we will keep her here and observe her continuously for a time, the doctor said."

She inquired if there would be damage because of the cocktail of drugs Amiha had taken.

The doctor assured her nothing would be life threatening or damaging at all. "Mrs. Kvad, is your daughter prone to attention seeking?"

"No. No, doctor. Amiha, has always been balanced, very well adjusted in all things."

"In all things," said the doctor. As if puzzled by 'in all things' comment Mommy stated.

"Does she need rest, doctor?" Aunt Cue asked.

"Yes, yes, she does, but she'll be wide awake for quite some time. Quite some time, indeed." As the doctor began to leave their presence he said, "You good people take a walk over to the lounge, and have a moment to rest yourselves. Everything will be just fine, and all is well."

They wondered if he was telling the truth.

Her mother spoke up and said, "Thank you kindly, Dr. Jones."

"You're welcome Mrs. Kvad. I'll take care of your daughter; nothing will happen to her, I won't let that happen. She has many assignments in life. Some will commence from today." And then he was off, just as he was never there.

Amiha's Mom, stared at the space Dr. Jones was just standing in and extended her right hand with her palm up, into the open air, and her hand turned beet red on the inside and became warm to the touch. She didn't say anything to her other family members. She simply closed her hand after a time, and moved on to the lounge room; while she felt her hand tingling.

Something had just happened, she knew, for she herself was an 'Angel of Light'. She had just encountered a higher evolved Angel. That's who Dr. Jones, Dr. Kantor Jones was. He was a Higher Evolved Angel of Light. He was her Guardian Angel, and now, he had been assigned to Amiha, for their Father's glory.

Amiha was 15 years old. She knew all of this, but she didn't really know this, she wondered how she knew that she knew and didn't know all at the same time.

"Oh well," she thought.

Stranger things than fiction happen... that's what Mommy always said.

The Beginning

✴

Laid out under the blinding hot sunshine of the Caribbean, cooled by the gentle breeze and beautiful crystal clear blue waters, Amiha felt totally at peace and content with all that was in her world, finally.

It had taken Amiha more than a lifetime to reach this point. There was something to be said for being patient and waiting on the Lord. Surely, if she had learned nothing else, she had learned patience; among a few other hundred lessons.

Amiha couldn't believe she had arrived on this beautiful island intact. She looked beyond fabulous. Her skin was flawless; however, it hadn't always been that way. Never had she even dared to reveal so much of herself.

MINISTER NELLIE A. WOSU

Black was her go-to New York color, with fierce red lipstick. Something had changed in her and it was more than evident. She was washed in color now; every jewel tone that existed, she wore it, neon or metalicized... which she highly favored.

Gleaming she was in plums, jade, red, coral, stark white, and every hue of blue one could imagine, and of course, orange and gold! Amiha was the new golden woman.

Adjusting her sunshades, Amiha stretched out on her beach chair in a tropical motif one-piece bathing suit that was cut in all of the most advantageous places. However, it was not whorish looking.

She was pleased that she had begun weight-lifting. She had stressed over aerobics, cycling, and the standard options to the fitness craze. With weight-lifting she saw results quicker and didn't have to cut back too much on her food intake. She had always been a healthy eater. Now, she was able to change the flab into fab. There was a distinct difference in the way her body was cut. She was proud of her hard work. Lord knows her trainer almost beat her into shape. It hadn't been easy, but here she was exactly ten months later and she was totally a different woman in every conceivable way.

Amiha relaxed, picked up her book and became engrossed in the hottest summer book, or so that was what was said about "Why Deny Yourself the Pleasure of a Forbidden Love".

Yes, friends, the go-to book "Why Deny Yourself the Pleasure of a Forbidden Love" was written by a little known somewhat insignificantly significant and obscure individual, who up until now had barely been known. That unknown was none other than Amiha Joye Kvad.

Amiha had found out that there's a difference between writing a book, and then reading the book one had written more than two years prior.

After having left the beach, showering, and getting a quick bite to eat in her suite, Amiha took a nap before she would dress and head down for the evening's dinner experience and whatever else would happen.

Amiha thought to herself that the fresh sea air will certainly relax and put you to sleep, quickly. Amiha had dozed off before her naturally bountiful head full of hair hit the beautiful white linens.

She inhaled and exhaled slightly as she went into a deep sleep; tossing and turning, once, twice, three times... and then on the fourth turn, she was right back there again, in future past.

Upon exiting the Justice Center, Amiha was hit with a barrage of members of the Press all saying simultaneously. 'Miss. Kvad, Miss. Kvad, tell us what happened?' Question after question was hurled at her.

She looked around to the left and to the right, afraid of the cameras and microphones being thrust into her face. Who were these people she thought? Blasted media hounds! She wanted to get out of here.

Just then, her attorney pulled her in close and said, "Miss. Kvad has no comment, please excuse us." Pushing through the crow, he protected her as he said he would. She let out a long sigh as he moved her along; blocking and defending her, in spite of the media hounds' myriad of accusations and innuendo. *God why has all of this happened to me? Is it my fault, she thought?*

Kantor D. Jones, Esq., attorney extraordinaire, he never loses, Amiha was told. He is the only one that you want to represent you. Kantor was Miss Kvad's attorney and her protector. He vowed to stick with her until all of this was all over with and still after that time, he swore that he would always be by her side come hell or high water.

It wasn't over yet and the high waters were rising at every turn. Slowly but surely, she began to believe what he said to her and to believe in him, too.

Kantor had told her to be strong; to go in and find herself. He told her she could get through all of this, if she wanted to. *Was that true? Did she even want it to be all over with?* Amiha didn't know what she wanted. She couldn't think of anything… she was simply numb. She barely knew when it had begun or how it had begun?

One thing she knew is that she wanted to sleep.

Kantor and a few of the Associates in his firm had taken her to a little-known restaurant where they could enjoy a bite to eat in private, peace, and quiet. Barely eating, she felt simple, wondering how she had caused all of this.

After dinner, everyone wished her well and continued to encourage her. Kantor was more than her attorney, he was a good friend. As they exited the restaurant, Kantor hummed a few bars, the sound was familiar. She couldn't quite recognize it, but she knew she had heard it before. Getting to his car, he gently stepped in front of her and opened the door for her. 'Your chariot awaits you'.

Shocked, she felt embarrassed. 'Well, enter in', so Amiha got in. He was such the capable individual, she used to feel that way; capable, before all of this. Kantor ensured she was strapped in. He closed her door. She waited for him to get in and said thank you and asked, "Do you do this for all of your clients?"

"Do this? What is this?"

She smiled just a little. "You know what I mean."

"If I did, I wouldn't ask the question."

Slightly rolling her eyes, she sighed as she shifted in her seat. He told her to put her seat back. The drive to Amiha's home was nearly two hours. She fell asleep in the luxurious *leather seats, listening to the music being played. Kantor looked over at Amiha from time to time. Then, he heard himself saying out quietly as a whisper, 'no, I don't, I only do this for you. Only you, ever.'*

"Amina, young lady you're home now. Let's get you inside so that you can get some rest and sleep for a change. Do not worry everything will be alright.

Amiha, Amiha, are you awake?"

Amiha stretched and rubbed her eyes while looking around, "Oh gee, we're here already?"

"Yep, we're here. Hang on, let me get your door and get you inside." Kantor carried Amiha's belongings up the stairs into her part of the home, looking around to see if all was in order.

It was. Then, he said, "I will call you tomorrow to see how you're doing. We have a conference being set up, which will bolster your image, and your story will be told.

She thanked him once again.

He looked at her and said, "I meant what I said. I will stand by you... do not worry."

She worried why he wasn't worried. Kantor was different somehow. "Thank you," she said once again.

Kantor shook his head, and smiled, "Do you ever say anything beyond 'Thank You'?"

"Yes," she said. "Thank you, Kantor, you're a blessing".

A fitting truth for her.

"Wonderful!" he said, turning and bidding her a good night; once again encouraging her to get some rest and sleep for a change.

Amiha showered and put her 'sleeping clothes' on, as her Aunt called pajamas or nightgowns. But first, she must 'cream her skin'. That's what her best friend Lucy called putting lotion on – 'creaming your skin'. Amiha thought, it's funny how folks from other places call things the strangest things.

She smiled and realized it was a genuine smile from her heart. They were with her. Saying her prayers, she started with the 'kiddy prayer'.

"Now I lay me down to sleep..."

[DREAM]

Hmmm good 'ol sleep, sleep that felt good, sleep that let you wake up refreshed, peaceful and full of joy, hope and new life. That's what she wanted she wanted new life! She imagined new life but couldn't see it at all, all she saw was gloom, lies, things being said that were twisted, mangled, untrue, manipulated and taken out of context. Everything that was beautiful had been relegated to the pit of nastiness and horrific sickness. Tossing and turning, tossing and turning, tossing and turning, tossing and turning, running out of breath, her throat was dry, burning, water running, running, running, running, gasping for air, heart pounding, falling down, looking up saying... "Father, forgive me, for I have sinned. Father, Father, Father do you hear me? FATHER she shouted, Forgive, me for I have sinned. 'Yes, child you have sinned. What shall be your penance?' 'Come sit and tell me what I want to hear', Father said. Tears running down her face she wept uncontrollably. Father agreed that she had sinned. But, what did Father do? Did he sin, too? Father was a towering and imposing figure, he was big, he was after all Father. He was her teacher. Wasn't he?

The familiar sound of Al Jarreau singing *Teach me Tonight* began to stir Amiha awake. She heard ♫"Starting with the ABC of it, right down to the XYZ of it, Graduation is almost here my love, teach me tonight. One thing isn't very clear, teach me tonight♫ **Amiha, Amiha, Amiha, Amiha teach ME tonight.**

Who, who is that?

That voice, that sound. Long sigh, rolling over, stretching and rubbing her eyes, she awakens. Wow, what kind of crazy dream was that? What time is it?

Squinting, Amiha's vision came clear.

Oh, it's 6:17 pm. Better get up and shower again before I dress for dinner. It looks like I've perspired. That's funny, the room doesn't feel too warm. Oh well, it's all good.

She looked around at her $450 per night suite. Father, who knew? Amiha's eyes went from left to right and back again. A chill fell over her and then nothing but silence.

Amiha got down on her knees and prayed the Sinners' Prayer. The Sinners' prayer is a prayer of repentance, prayed by individuals who feel convicted of the presence of sin in their lives and have the desire to form or renew a personal relationship with God through Jesus Christ... *Lord have mercy on me, Lord have mercy on me, Christ have mercy on me. No weapon formed against me shall prosper in Jesus' holy name.* Amen.

Selah.

Amiha stayed on her knees for a moment longer thanking God Almighty for His hedge of protection. Then, she got up and sang, *I Run to You,* sung by Whitney Houston in the movie 'The Preacher's Wife'. Amiha loved that song most of all. She ran to the shower and sang that song to the top of her lungs while she showered, toweled off, and creamed her skin!

Yep, she sure did!

Amiha showered and dressed her curvaceous self in a flowing gown made in colors of the waters; shades of sheer blues with just a hint of periwinkle. The underdress was made of shimmering gold, her sandals were golden and blue with rhinestones. It looked as if she was walking in diamonds.

Her jewelry was understated with impact; make-up minimal, lips afire in liquid gold with undertones of barely there pinks. Amiha's hair was gorgeous and bountiful; she had had it colored in shades of golden apricot, sun-kissed raisin and auburn, about a month prior so her hair was not brassy, but warm. Her hair had a natural wave pattern; it could be silky straight with just a bit of heat or it could be like it was now, loose-flowing and swept to the side, cascading, and brushing against her smooth honey brown skin.

And, of course, as would be expected, her fragrance was compellingly sultry, yet light and lingering; the impact of her scent was not caught until she had passed.

That's when heads would turn.

Entering at what seemed to be just the precise time of day so that the setting sun featured her, she saw those looking at her as she walked in. She waited to be noticed by the Maître 'D so she could be seated.

Amiha always dined alone.

When Amiha entered into the Pavilion, there was an unmistaken hush. Voices that were busily engaged in laughter, and orders being taken by the wait staff, suddenly had become undeniably silenced.

A FORBIDDEN LOVE

Amiha was totally unaware that she was the cause of the stoppage of sound; heads turning to look, gaze if you will, upon her! Of all people, Amina! So shocked was she that she stopped too, in dead stride to look to see who had entered and caused the silence to become silent.

"Good evening, Madame", said Gustav, the Maître 'D in that luscious and vibrantly baritone tinged with just the slightest bit of seduction in his voice.

Amiha was immediately taken aback. Madame? Amiha thought, me married? Humph! Nah, Dude that's not for me. I don't think so. Humph, again. Of course, these were all her own thoughts.

A mere moment had passed.

"Madame, will someone be joining you or shall you dine alone this evening?"

"Alone, thank you."

Gustav smiled politely and nodded thinking to himself, 'what foolish man would leave such a lovely and exquisite being to dine alone?' American men in their treatment of their women baffled him. Gustav led Amiha to a central table where she wouldn't be too exposed, but where she also would be seen, by him. He smiled to himself when he asked Amiha if this table was suitable for Madame.

She smiled and said, "it's quite suitable, indeed. Thank you." Like the expert that he was, he pulled out the chair and waited for her to slip into the chair comfortably, before he slipped the chair up to the table at just the precise distance.

Yes, Gustav knew his business well.

Amiha smiled broadly as she settled back in her chair. This was an excellent table, choice, even. At that moment, the waiter appeared with the menu, introducing himself as *Jaime* and asking what she would like to drink.

"Sparkling water with a twist, Jaime."

"Very good Mademoiselle. I'll be right back."

Lowering her eyelids, Amiha glanced at the menu, considering what her palate would delight in this evening.

Amiha was starting to feel something changing moment by moment in her breathing; meaning her living. She was very grateful and humbled by it all.

Only God, only God. Thank you.

Dining Alone

✺

The appetizer of gazpacho and cucumber with a hit of dill had been served.

"Mademoiselle your meal has been prepared just as you requested," said Jaime, beaming with pride, as if he had prepared the meal himself. As he rolled the serving cart to her, eyes and noses were stretched wide to see just what this lovely woman was about to dine on.

What had she ordered? While every dish at the Pavilion was delectable, this they hadn't seen on the menu. The aroma of the medium to near well-done sliced beef was garlic-rubbed with zesty infused olive oil (just barely a dab) and then sautéed in a fabulous Bordeaux reduction with shallots, wild greens, Vidalia onions, and mushrooms; served with sweet potato and hot peppers... all of which was second to none.

To the side, were three small redskin potatoes, topped with cool relish and just a dab of fresh butter for the flatbread made in a cast iron skillet that appeared to be one layer, but was actually four layers of the lightest and flakiest crust imaginable.

Jaime sat a small cup next to Amiha's dinner plate. There was something in it. But what? Amiha looked at the food approvingly and let her senses take in the beauty of this feast for her palate, eyes, and nostrils.

She smiled, nodding in approval.

Jaime standing there waiting for Amiha to say something, anything. She smiled demurely and looked up at him, saying "Thank you." She blushed to herself thinking of Kantor asking her so long ago, 'is there anything else you can say?' Oh, Amiha could say very much; yes, she sure could and had done just that. Speech can be so liberating when it is spoken in and with truth.

Amiha took her napkin and spread it in her lap and then bowing her head, Amiha said prayer over her food.

A FORBIDDEN LOVE

She always gave thanks even in tribulations. She was most thankful for the myriad of meals He had prepared for her in the presence of her enemies. She invited her enemies to dine with her. They could not eat in her presence any longer, for they were her footstool. But, still she invited them to come partake of what the Lord had prepared for everyone.

Smiling, she lifted the small cup and took three sips. She pursed her lips... squinting her eyes somewhat while doing so.

Then, she took up her butter knife, spread a half a pat of butter on the flatbread, taking a bite of the bread; again taking three sips from that little cup, she shifted in her seat, and began to enjoy a meal that was totally decadent!

As her Aunt would say, 'make you lose your tongue'. Aunt Nova would love this whole vibe! She lived on this scale all the time from way before 'back in the day' had arrived.

This was her! Now, it was Amiha! God did it!

Jaime had returned to the table a few times to see if there was anything that Amiha needed. Each time, she had said all was in order. She didn't fidget with her phone like other diners who dined alone were doing. She was completely at peace with dining just by herself.

Occasionally, Amiha would notice from her peripheral that some were stealing glances. She would look up, smile, and nod. Once she even lifted up her glass as in toast to a group at the opposite table and said, "Salut!"

Oh, Amiha was truly having the time of her life!

Gustav had been watching Amiha, without ever looking. He had passed her in seating others and nodded in his worldly manner saying "Madame" all in one movement. His form and movement was fluid and quick, but not herkie jerky. He was confident and smooth without being a lothario. She even overheard him speaking in several languages.

Where was he from, she wondered.

This island paradise was not frequented by the mainstream travelers who went to the Caribbean. This island was likened unto a Reality Fantasy Paradise Island. With its white and pink sand beaches, the water was like diamonds that were crystal clear, but beautiful shades of blue and green. When the sun began to set much later than would be expected, the island took on another form; that of an idyllic life as in a hidden protected garden.

There were many people here, yet it never seemed overcrowded. The voices, which were many, were happy and filled with laughter, song, and the most incredible music this side of heaven. Everything sounded light and peaceful; like everyone was speaking different languages, which seemed familiar to Amiha's ears.

Amiha marveled at her childlike excitement.

Suddenly Gustav was standing at her side, he was so very tall. She felt as a small child with him standing there right next to her.

Where had he come from so quickly?

"Madame Kvad, would you like dessert now or shall I deliver it to your room later?"

What? Is he talking to me? Deliver dessert to my room... him? Wait a minute buddy? It's not that type of game.

For the first time, her face wasn't smiling.

No, she didn't use the Aunt Cue, death-ray stare, she just sat still.

Him, not to be outdone, stood waiting for her response. "Madame Kvad are you alright?"

Hell no, you're all wrong, dude! Long sigh (internal) here we go, "Yes, I am all right. You were saying something, sir?"

Gustav continued to stand even the more erect as she looked up to him. Her neck was nearly bent in a backward L.

Damn 90°degree angle... she was more flexible these days; however, she was NOT a contortionist.

Now, Amiha wished Kantor were here with her.

A gentleman's gentleman.

Where did this jack... before she could finish her thought, Gustav said, "Madame Kvad, you... you, look," then he took an external long sigh, and finished "You look as if you've finished your meal. Perhaps dessert is not your desire at this time, is that it?"

Feeling defeated, Amiha was at a loss for words; quite an unusual occurrence for her. "Ah, no, that's fine. I'll have my dessert now, in the open garden."

"Excellent... and very good. The breeze is beautiful this evening," said Gustav.

And just like that, he slid her chair back, nodded and seemed to have lifted the chair off the floor, without her feeling being settled back to the ground.

What kind of man is this?

At that moment, he took her hand, and escorted her to the open garden. Everyone looked at Gustav and Amiha. Amiha caught their reflection in the mirror as they went out to the open garden, but she couldn't see him, for he was so very tall. She could only see his torso.

As he led her to the open garden he engaged her in small talk; which was more than small. She hesitated as they entered into the garden; the last views of the sun were setting fast. The sky was pinks, purples, and slivers of gold joining the extended waters which were now indigo.

Totally breathtaking was this live view.

He said "Is there something wrong? You've stopped." Do you no longer wish to have your dessert here?"

She blinked, still lovely as ever. She managed a half smile.

"No, not at all. I just am not too familiar with being outside so much, especially when it's dark," Amiha managed to say; albeit sounding somewhat withdrawn.

"Madame Kvad, do you fear the dark or darkness?" he asked, seeming genuinely concerned.

She paused. *No, not any more,* she thought to herself.

"There are no serpents of any type here, Madame Kvad. only love, light, and beautiful butterflies."

How did he know what was on my mind, she wondered? Amiha asked, "None at all?"

"My dear lady, there are absolutely none, and never will be for that matter."

How could he be so sure? This was an island.

He read her mind and answered her internal question, "Because that's the way it has been written. All serpents have been banished and burn in hell. There is absolutely nothing to fear at this elevation."

Elevation?

Once again Amiha marveled, she was at peace again and glowed in this surreal light. She was truly magnificent; feeling foolish to think that this kind man was trying to rub her the right/wrong way or wrong/right way.

At that moment, they both looked up and saw Jaime on his way with many others in tow, all with smiles on their faces, as the wait staff brought out the dessert for everyone, the very dessert she had requested; strawberries, peaches, chocolate cream with apricots and Grand Marnier.

Amiha laughed out loud, as did everyone, sitting in this most beautiful of places, a circle of familial love eating her favorite dessert! Gustav, Jaime, and Amiha looked at each other and began eating; smiling and enjoying this special night.

Amiha thought she was on the come up.

Jaime said, "You're more than that Amiha, you *are* the come up!"

What?! How did he hear that? Me... the come up?

Years prior, perhaps a decade or more, Amiha vaguely remembered saying to a work colleague that he was smarter than all of his colleagues; including his boss. He was just biding his time to learn how the game was played. This colleague's wife was disabled and a bit of a bothersome pain, Amiha thought.

She thought the wife, albeit disabled, could do more.

In any event, her colleague didn't want to admit that truth, nor did he want to admit to being the smartest in the group. He did not have an attitude with a cocky manner, he just was graced with this knowledge. When Amiha said "Hey, you're the game here, right, aren't you, not them?" The man's face drained of all color and then his face turned beet-red.

Yes, Amiha had nailed it yet again. She knew. She didn't know how she knew... but she knew. She always knew.

So why had Jaime said, she was the 'Come up'?

Positioning, that is why.

Amiha knew her position, but had never truly embraced it... there is perhaps for some, such a thing as being too humble. Inwardly she queried, 'Is that not so, Father?'

Father didn't respond to her question. At least, not in the present moment. But he would. He always did.

As the evening lingered, it became even lovelier. The music filled the warm gentle breeze like a blanket of comfort that was made of the finest silks filled with color. Everything in this place was colorful and rich.

The likes of which Amiha had never seen.

Her eyes, her sight, filled with what seemed to be beyond 20/20; if that were possible. What seemed to Amiha was that her "vision" had become magnificent. she could see miles away, or so she thought.

This island was a dreamscape.

Soon everyone had paired off and began dancing; Lovers embracing, bending over, and placing the sweetest of kisses of all, the forehead kiss, on their partner's faces.

Amiha stared longingly. She had had a love that placed kisses on her forehead too. She exhaled slightly and felt a tremor move throughout her being. At that moment, the tremor was interrupted by Jaime coming to her hurriedly, saying "Mademoiselle, mademoiselle, mademoiselle, there's someone here to see you!"

"Me?"

"Yes, you!"

Why was Jaime so excited? Who could be here to see her? She stammered, and almost frightened asked, "who is here to see me, Jaime?"

By now, the evening was over, and all was well, except Amiha had not learned who was there to see her. Apparently, whoever was here had to depart abruptly and said that they would return before long.

How long was before long?

No one indicated if the individual was a male or a female. She didn't like the way this was moving. What was happening? Everything had been perfect until this shit had come up.

However, no one had seemed it to be a bad situation; with only the one exception... Amiha herself. Amiha didn't like surprises. No, she never did, unless it was a birthday party for her. And, even then, she wanted to know, so she could prepare herself to look good and surprised when they yelled 'SURPRISE!'.

Back in her room, Amiha changed for the evening, with her shower already over, she settled into the California King, reached over and turned out the light. "Thank you Lord for this day, I love you, Father, Son and Holy Ghost. Please forgive me of all of my sins; known or unknown, and protect my family in everything that matters today and beyond. In Jesus' holy name...

Amiha, thought she picked up her book... yes, that book, the hottest book of the summer, and began to thumb through the pages; searching out where she had left off earlier, when she was on the beach..

Before, she realized, she became engrossed in deep sleep, but a disturbing sleep.

[DREAM]

Tell us how it began, how long had this been going on? When did you know? Questions, questions, questions and more questions. With every question Amiha had on less clothing. Kantor was advising her of something, but what? Seemed as if he were saying: 'Tell only the truth. Make up nothing. There's nothing for you to be ashamed of." But, wasn't' there something to be ashamed of? How could she tell the truth?

In her mind, she remembered she heard her mother saying to her in so many of the life lessons, "Amiha, the truth will stand and a lie will fall. Tell the truth even if it makes you look bad for if you tell the truth, some may have mercy on you.

She needed so much mercy and more, she needed and wanted this crap to be over with. How could she have allowed herself to get this far in? Wasn't anyone honorable anymore?

From way over to the left, she heard a voice, 'Certainly there are honorable people in the world, you're one of them, aren't you?'

Amiha thought she was, but she was as a filthy rag.

Baby you ain't no rag, and there is nothing filthy about you, you're clean and pure like being untouched, but if you want to get sullied let's... pregnant pause... then that laugh that filled her head and her body, making her arch her back.

Amiha thrashed about in the California King bed with the neon white sheets, everything was white with exception of the back support, which was sorta navy blue or gray, she couldn't tell. But there it sat upon the bed like a judgment seat.

And, of course, there was the tribunal in the other left corner, the 23 pairs of shoes, lined up like a firing squad, they were going to shoot her ass, and that was all there was too, it.

And, at that time, she fell backwards, and screamed in total abandon and that voice with the wonderful pitch, came out and said baby, say it for me, go ahead say it for me.

Amiha, heard the questions growing louder where did you meet? How did you, well how did you like being his? He felt her up again, and began fondling her breast, he loved breasts, he loved her breast more than all, he had said, they were firm, and soft, and he, began suckling her breast like a new born baby starving for the milk. My word, girl, you know how to get me there.

Get him where? What was he talking about?

How many times did you die?

Ugh, I died, air escaped from her open mouth. Miss Kvad, we've told you, you must answer the questions. We need to know, what happened? What happened, what happened, what happened?

I-I-I-I don't know.

YOU don't know?

No, I don't know!

How could YOU not know?

Well, she twisted uncomfortably in her chair, and said, 'it was so long ago.' It was becoming increasingly difficult to deal with this. Kantor, said to tell the truth. But, why, tell the truth, it was over, it was done with. Wasn't it?

Come on baby, tell me what I want to hear, say it for me, you know what I want and need to complete this, say it for me, then he slid and began to say it and call her name, Amiha, Amiha, you belong to me, don't you? Well, do you?

It was hard to hear what he was saying, because all of these questions were being hurled at her in her head, and at her head, he was so very tall, it was hard to see him at times.

He found new ways to hide from her and then he'd pop up and that was all there was. Come on say it for me, he pressed her, repeatedly, he continued to press and suckle the twins, kneading and needin; there he was and the questions were everywhere, all over everywhere, voices coming faster than light don't let me down baby, what is it I want from you?

My joy father, my joy, and then he pumped her for more, what is it, his voice was so beautiful and yes, he was beautiful, too. Cocoa smooth, straight black hair, hands softer than hers almost. Then he smacked playfully on the bum and said baby did good. So, if baby did good, why did baby, feel like, she had just been placed in the judgment seat?

He said you got a 10 baby, you always do. He didn't kiss her, ever, he burrowed himself in her neck or cleavage.

All rise, the honorable Judge Calliston presiding...

Just then, Kantor said, 'don't worry, I am here with you and nothing and no one no one is going to harm you, I'll see to that. He kept flitting his tongue, ever so slightly in and out, he never used to do that, she thought.

What's wrong here?

The stench of urine, with a top note of Pine-Sol, was in her nostrils. She thought it might be on the seats. Amiha was concerned that her clothes would smell like him and this pissy chair. Then he beckoned for her to come over and sit next to him. Damn it to hell. And, she wretched, how many years has this been going on?

How many, tell us how many Miss Kvad. When did it begin? We NEED to know and you're the only one who can shed light on this. Most others are dead.

She tightened up. Kantor was there and gave her the approving sign; she exhaled, as if for the first time in her life. She raised her lowered head, adjusted her back, her mother was there, too… and so were many others.

Who were they?

They were her relatives, and no one was angry with her, their faces beamed with love.

MINISTER NELLIE A. WOSU

Miss Kvad, Miss Kvad, when did this begin?

She wanted to protect him, her father; for she had always loved him in some manner. Your testimony will set others free. 'Set others free?' She had never thought of it like that. She had never been truly free of this, it had changed her. It was like, being in and out at the same time.

She heard in her head Janis Joplin singing and saying ♫Freedom is just another word for nothing left to lose, nothing don't mean nothing honey if it ain't free, and feeling good was easy Lord when he sang the blues, you know feeling good was good enough for me, good enough for me and MY, [Amiha had changed the lyric from Bobby McGee to *"father".,* she *continued to hear, say and believe, that father, had shared the secrets of her soul (and he opened his to her) for he had said to her too many times that she was the only one who didn't bore him] the song continued in her head ♪through all kinds of weather, through everything they'd done....♪*

So it was this dream sequence, that she never wanted to have played out, as she tossed and tossed, and tossed some more. Somewhere she felt this was not about what had been done to her, it was about what was forbidden and the twisted mangled seduction of it all; a coming of age.

She wasn't quite old enough to understand, but oh, she did understand. It would take years for the 'situation' to be actualized, but for now Amiha simply swallowed her disgrace, her secret, her sullied honor, and sat up straight, and pushed her back into the chair and said 'It began, when I was, when I was 15 years old."

The bottom fell out, there it was, finally out, the booth that she sat in hadn't dropped her in the abyss of degradation and filth. She said it out loud and released what she feared; telling that story.

Neckties were adjusted, and a few ahems were heard.

Nevertheless, Amiha was still there, standing.. or in this case, sitting.

Or, so she thought she was.

Then she saw through the graying, grayish navy blue, back erector for reading in her bed, her bed, the flickering tongue, ever so slightly, ever so slightly, that tongue, would exit and enter, exit, and enter the mouth. She heard 'Baby tell me what I want to hear, tell me baby what I need to hear, come wash me, come wash me', she heard that beautiful voice say, but now the voice was not as booming.

It had taken on a different tone, a type of weakness, and there he was, pushing her back, way back, for he was so very tall... 'hold it, hold it, hold it a minute', he said, and released the fire inside of his tortured and sick soul.

Amiha woke up screaming. "FATHER, forgive me, for I have sinned, again."

Wake up child, wake up, what, what?

The pages of the book Amiha had been reading, her book, were crumpled. The light in her room was still on... hadn't she turned off the lights? Why was this book in her hands crumpled up?Too many questions, too many questions and who had come to see her? Who was it?

Jesus, was she losing her mind?

The Truth Revealed

Rolling over, stretching like a kitten, Amiha squinted. The sun was beaming through the windows of Amiha's suite. It was literally a blinding, white, golden light. As she came out of her sleep, she felt she had been running all night and working out.

She had slept and fallen into a deep sleep.

By that moment, there was a knock at the door. "Mademoiselle," she heard a delicate voice say.

"Yes, who is it?"

"Room service," said the voice.

"Room service?"

"Oui."

Amiha opened the door, after peering through the peephole.

This lovely, seemingly older, but young woman, entered; pushing a beautiful breakfast. She had a beautiful smile, that when she smiled the room became brighter.

"Bonjour petit, et commet vas-tu? Je vais bien."

At that time, Amiha could have sworn she heard another voice say, *"she's always fine."* Amiha looked around to see if there was someone else in the room.

Nope, no one there.

Amiha said, "I didn't order room service for this morning."

The seemingly older, but lovely young woman smiled and said, "Breakfast is the most important meal of the day."

What? Amiha thought to herself. *Mommy always said that.* The seemingly older, but lovely young woman smiled again, and the room lit up with sunlight even the more! *I need to get my eyes checked.*

And, the seemingly older, but lovely young woman said, "There's nothing wrong with your vision."

What the...?

The woman looked at Amiha and said, "Pray without ceasing, and prayers work and change many things... yes, they do, and they always will do just that, change things. For those that love the Lord and are called according to His purpose. All things are new again, like before, the before, Amiha. I made this breakfast for you, just you Kitten."

Kitten? Stunned, Amiha said, "My daddy used to call me Kitten, and he called my Mommy..."

"Kitten Britches."

Amiha just about lost her balance. The woman reached out and caught her before she hit the floor.

Her eyes and heart opened, she asked, "Ma? Mommy, Mommy, is that you? Could this be, where am I Mommy? You died decades ago? What is this all about? Mommy what is this all about?"

"But I live now, my daughter. I live now."

"Mommy, did I die? Am, I dead, Mommy?"

No, Amiha, you're alive and living for His glory. You passed all of your tests. You told the truth, and so you live the new life of all life."

"Mommy, it's been like a dream, and sometimes, I was not happy, and sometimes they lied on me; they treated me like crap do-do. They hated me Mommy. They left me! They left me!"

"Amiha, they were supposed to leave you. They were on assignment too. Just like you have been since you were seven years old. You said, you'd go, and so you did go. And you left others, too. Amiha you've never been alone. You traveled with Father on the path He set before you. You gave, you took, but most of all, you loved, shared, and forgave. Your tally was summed up and you've done good for the heart of many."

Amiha began to cry.

"No, no Amiha. There are no tears here. No sorrow."

"Mommy, where are we?"

"Amiha, we're in Paradise High!" Amiha's Mommy replied, laughing and glowing radiantly.

"Paradise High? Where is that Mommy?"

"It's where you belong Amiha."

"But, Ma, I have written books, I've worked as a technology professional, I've, I've..."

"Yes, yes Amiha, you've done much, but you've always done everything for God's glory in His Son's name, haven't you? Amiha, you look puzzled? What's wrong?"

"Mommy, I've done wrong things too. Too many wrong things," Amiha said, hanging her head. "I've done shameful things, Ma. Horrifically, shameful things."

"Amiha, your heart has been burdened and labored for several life-times. You fought the good fight of faith; you were true to God always. Some didn't understand, but you did. And, you continued to try, despite much travail."

Amiha wondered, "Is this heaven?"

"No, not yet. It's a type of foyer to heaven," Amiha.

"Mommy, they put me on trial about Father."

"Yes, they did, and rightly so. Not because of what you did, but for what he did. Father was to teach you the Word, not use you for his sexual deviant behaviors."

"Ma, but he didn't. He didn't do anything to me."

"He did more than anything to you, Amiha. He did you. He changed you, but your heart was young and pure, and you did something to him, too."

Amiha sank back and lowered her head.

"No... hold your head high, for when he came at you with that dirty lustful spirit, you resisted. Father had become angry, and didn't do what he was supposed to do with you; to love you and keep you. He was to be your husband. He and his indiscretions were too foul and the number of women he betrayed.

However, he did love you. It's a good thing that you were able to make the escape as you did. Remember, your Father in heaven will always make a way of escape for you, when you are tempted. You resisted the devil and crushed his head. Now, you're alive again, that was just about the last test you were to take.

There were more, but you, having gained strength by being in the valley, left you openly receptive to living only for the Lord. Thus, today is the day when your heart's desire is given to you."

All at once, Amiha's heart beat wildly and she inhaled deeply and as her eyes opened, she saw, for the first time, her beloved, Kantor D. Jones.

Then, her Mommy said to her, "This is your life's love, Amiha. This is Michael, your true Loving Angel of Light. He's always been with you, as many others were for a time. He was John, he was Joseph, and he was your husbands, too. He's been your Guardian Angel; sent by God to keep you company, and your love renewed.

He is your friend.

His mother has always prayed for you Amiha. Do you remember that she told you that if she had had a daughter, that she would want her to be just like you?

Well her desire is fulfilled also.

Amiha, you belong to your Father, and He's shared you with all of us. He's given you much, and you've endured much; even beyond measure, for times beyond times even known. You've not been perfect, but you have been perfected in loving your Father in Heaven and placing none before Him. You've taught love and you've encouraged even your enemies.

So, now in this place, Paradise High, you get to live as one with your Guardian Angel, Michael, as Kantor D. Jones'. He was here to see you, and had to take care of some things, quickly. He's on a mission assignment for kingdom purposes and he'll return again to you after a time. He always does. Sometimes he gets held up, but he will always return.

Do you recall, what Gustav said to you last evening, that this elevation, there are no snakes?"

Amiha thought back and said "Yes, Mommy."

"Right. The enemy burns in hell, so there are no snakes in Paradise High, Heaven, or Heavenly places. This is for the elect Lady and her children. This is for us Amiha! Do you believe Amiha that your life has been changed?"

"Yes, Mommy. I believe that my heart has been changed and no one can change the path that I must go. I believe what I feel and no one can change that. I am His and He is mine. My life, my new life, is for His glory."

Amiha started to ascend a beautiful staircase that appeared before her. She could hear voices cheering and welcoming her; saying, *We knew you would make it. Come on up, we've been waiting for you. You're right on time...*

Welcome.

Amiha climbed the stairs without difficulty; noting to herself that as each step became higher and higher, she was not out of breath. She was breathing freely, and she was happier beyond ever.

Amiha had made it, with a little help from a heart that was bigger than life itself!

Amiha was free forever more.

She rejoiced as she heard, "Well done, enter in."

Epilogue

The alarm went off and Amiha awoke, rubbing her eyes. With a start she gasped, "Good grief, it's September First. Oh Lord, the story hasn't been completed yet, and Desireé is waiting for it!

Gosh, whew! Oh, thank you Jesus, for this beautiful day; in each and every way."

Amiha reached for her Bible, and when she did, out fell a card. *What is this?* "Wow, I thought I had filed all of these business cards. How is this one still here?"

Looking at the card, she pondered aloud, "Who in the world is a Kantor D. Jones? Isn't that something to do with the Altar stuff in Church?"

Oh well, whatever.

A FORBIDDEN LOVE

"Gotta hit it hard and fast to get this story finished now. I don't have time for this; it's already late! What's the title of the story going to be? Hmmm, 'A Forbidden Love'.

Nah, nah.

Thinking of her forbidden loves, Amiha stared into space and tried to think of the first words to put onto the blank piece of paper in front of her.

The phone began ringing, ringing, ringing...

Amiha sighed and hit the speaker button. "Hello?"

"Hi Amiha, this is Kantor Jones, I am back finally, and this time for good. I've been missing you and only you. Let me take you out to breakfast, lunch, and dinner for the rest of our lives, together.

Amiha fell back on the bed. "Jesus!"

Kantor smiled and said, "That's just what He said you would say."

They both laughed!

To everyone... just wait on the Lord!

A Divine Twist of Fate

BOOM!

The loud explosion woke Vivian from her sleep.

She, and her husband Rob, lived on the penthouse floor of a Chicago high-rise with just the normal chaos. Nothing like this had ever occurred in their 15 years of living downtown.

They had moved from Atlanta to Chicago after Rob had accepted a job with a new firm; Vivian quickly attaining a position with a company, since she had already garnered a remarkable reputation as an editor and publisher, while living in Atlanta.

She ran to the window to see what was going on, and saw people scurrying everywhere . . . thick clouds of smoke filled the air and sirens were blaring.

It appeared that the building next door had exploded and gone up in flames, but she couldn't really tell.

Running back to the room to awaken Rob and tell him what was going in – right at that moment - the doorman called on the apartment intercom and advised that their building was being evacuated also. He stated that the entire downtown area was surrounded by police and bomb squad personnel.

She went to wake up Rob. "Rob we have to leave the building and the area. There has been an explosion next door. Our building is being evacuated also. We have to get out."

They got dressed and took what they could and proceeded to head downstairs. Of course, they could not take the elevators, so they had to walk down the 12 flights of stairs.

What a calamity! Vivian thought. "What in the world could be going on?" She asked Rob.

They both were bewildered.

Chicago is a rough city to live in, yet they had always loved living here because of their businesses, community, and political affiliations.

Chicago is enmeshed with culture and vibrancy; a beautiful city.

Vivian was the Sr. Editor of a mainstream publishing company and worked in the heart of downtown Chicago, about two blocks from their condominium.

Rob was a Sr. Partner at one of the largest law firms in the area. They had strong ties to the community and were considered among the elite; both community activists and belonging to several civic organizations as well as cultural groups. They had done well financially, and traveled the world, yet did not have any children. Even though Vivian wanted kids Rob always dismissed the idea.

Neither of them was overly religious, but had attended church a few times together; lately Rob had been traveling much more for the firm out of state and Vivian had gotten really swamped at work, so their lives were seemingly "distant."

She still had hoped to have kids. Rob was loving and supportive of her dreams, but was always disconnected when the conversation of children came up.

Finally, they got downstairs and were able to see all of the commotion going on. Mass pandemonium filled the streets of downtown Chicago and people were running everywhere; screaming and injured.

The building next to their high-rise had collapsed and all they saw were people screaming and crying.

It was horrible.

Vivian gasped, "Oh my God Rob! What is going on? What is happening?"

There were police directing everyone to get to shelter if possible. "Call and check on your family members," yelled someone in the distance. "Someone has ordered a bomb threat on all of the downtown area and we need to get you out of here."

Just then Rob remembered that he had left his briefcase, a large sum of cash and bonds in their safe, along with his wallet upstairs. He had their computers and devices, they had thrown into a bag several clothing items and things that they could grab quickly and ran out, but he forgot to get those items. He told Vivian to go to the parking deck and get in the car; he would be right back.

Vivian said, "No Rob. We need to go, please don't go back in there."

He assured her, "It will be okay. I need to make sure that we are okay to travel and be able to get somewhere to stay while this chaos dies down. I'll be okay. I'll be right back. Head to the car and meet me back here."

Vivian ran to the parking deck to get their SUV and meet him near the front entrance.

Fighting his way through the crowd of people and smoke, Rob headed back into the building. Before he made it to the stairs, someone had yelled, "BOMB! There's another bomb!"

BOOM!

Suddenly there was another blast – from out of nowhere. Vivian turned around and screamed, "ROB!"

Their building burst into flames and began falling to the ground. "OH MY GOD," Vivian yelled. "ROB, ROB...."

She looked around and seeing some police officers, she screamed, "Officers, my husband just went back in the building. Please tell me he's okay! Please tell me he's okay!"

"Ma'am, you can't go in there."

"Please… You don't understand. He went back in to get some things we had forgotten. Please tell me he's okay!"

"Ma'am, we are unable to tell right now if he's okay."

Vivian looked up to the sky and cried out to God for the first time in years, "Lord, please let my husband be okay. Please let him be okay."

As she stood there watching the building burn to the ground, she realized there was nothing she could do. Her beloved husband was inside that burning building and there was nothing she could do. "Oh my God, my husband. My husband. Rob."

At that very moment Vivian knew in her heart that Rob was not going to make it out of that explosion alive. It was too devastating. The blast was enormous and totally unexpected. There just were not enough police and bomb intervention specialists to handle this level of devastation. The scene was almost as bad as 9-1-1 had been years before.

Tears flooded Vivian's face. She couldn't get her thoughts together. All she could think was that the love of her life was inside that building and probably dead.

As she continued to stand there, stunned and crying, an older lady came up to her and began comforting her. One of the emergency medical team members brought over a blanket to wrap around her and asked her some questions. "Ma'am is there anyone we can call for you?"

Vivian heard her speaking, but the words sounded jumbled and distant. Finally she came to herself and asked, "What did you say?"

"Is there anyone we can call for you? Do you have any family... children?"

Vivian said, "My family is in South Carolina. My husband's family is in Atlanta. I have to look up phone numbers. I just want to make sure my husband is okay first. When will I know if he's okay? No... we don't have any children."

Vivian was in shock.

The medical team offered to take her to the hospital. Vivian replied, "No.... no, I am fine. I just want to make sure Rob is okay."

Just then the building attendant approached Vivian and said, "Ms. Challis.... I am so sorry. I am so sorry. He didn't make it. I am so sorry. I tried to stop him from going upstairs because the officers said it was not safe. But, he wouldn't listen. He kept saying he would be okay. At that moment the officers rushed me out. All of the other tenants and staff made it out safely from what we can tell. But he wouldn't listen. I am so sorry."

He kept apologizing.

Vivian just screamed and fell to the ground. She couldn't believe it. She was devastated. Her world was crumbling right there in those few moments. Just hours ago they were resting and life was good and now her heart was being ripped apart. Never before had she encountered this magnitude of despair and trauma.

EMT's rushed past. The fire fighters finally had gotten the flames to a controlled state; the sound of sirens still blaring.

Vivian felt like the world was spinning around her. She was numb. She couldn't move. She heard the voices, she saw the people, but everything was so distant. It would take hours, perhaps days before the area would be cleared.

The EMT's helped her get to a place of safety and she contacted her best friend, Liz. She was able to get a hotel several miles from the site of the accident. Rob had a stellar reputation in the community and high integrity when it came to financial matters, so she knew she wouldn't have to worry about any of that. It was just everything was inside their home.

The memories... Everything.

Starting over was the most difficult thing for her to process right now. She needed to make so many phone calls, yet she could not contain her thoughts. However, she knew the right people to help her regain focus would be her best friends, Liz and her husband, Charles.

Liz and Charles lived in Greenville, South Carolina, which is where Vivian was from. Liz never really worked a career, although she was highly educated.

She mostly volunteered and organized community events for her husband's business and their church. Charles had built a successful and wealthy business for them over the years and Liz' family was independently wealthy from farming and establishing businesses along the coast of South Carolina.

Several rings and then Vivian heard Liz pick up the phone, and Liz heard Vivian sobbing. "Viv, what's wrong?"

"Liz, have you seen the Chicago news?"

Liz said, "No. I have been at a church organizational meeting today. What's wrong Viv? You're scaring me."

"Liz. Rob is gone. He's dead. He was killed in an explosion that happened in our building earlier this morning. I don't know what to do. I don't know where to go right now."

"Vivian, oh my Father in heaven... Vivian I am so sorry!"

Dead silence. Liz was crying with her. She called Charles to the phone and told him what happened.

Charles and Rob had become best friends over the years. They had an upcoming trip to go fishing out in Oregon later in the year.

Charles took over the call. "Vivian... you can come here for a few days until you sort out what you need to do.

I am sure that you will want to speak with Rob's family in person and you will need help with everything. We will go with you to Atlanta if necessary. Just let us know."

Vivian replied, "Thank you Charles. I am going to stay here just a couple of days to meet with his firm and get some things in order. I have a hotel nearby and I know that I will be okay financially. I just need to sort everything out. I will probably have a memorial here and one in Atlanta."

By this time Vivian's phone began to ring.

"My phone is ringing. It's Rob's mother."

She had not had time yet to contact anyone else. CNN, Chicago news stations, and every other major news channel in the United States had already reported the story.

Her phone was ringing and she did not know what to say. She had wanted to tell everyone in person; however, it was too late. How in the world was she going to tell her over the phone that her son was gone?

So, she answered the phone.

"Vivian... is everything okay there in Chicago? I saw that there was a major explosion downtown. How are you and Rob?"

In between sobs she began to explain, "Mother, there was an explosion next to our building early this morning and we were advised to evacuate the condo. We pulled together as much as we could, but we forgot some things, and Rob went back inside our building to get them. That's when the second explosion took place. He didn't make it back out."

Rob's mother screamed, "Oh my God... my son. Oh my God. Why Lord? Why my son?"

In the background, Vivian heard the screams from other family members who were around.

"Mother Challis... I am so sorry. I asked him not to go back in. He wouldn't listen. I am so sorry."

The phone beeped. It was Vivian's mother.

She explained to Rob's mom that she would be there in a few days because she wanted to hold a service there first. "Mother I am making plans to come there in a few days. I wanted to tell everyone in person, but that's not possible now. I have to sort some things out here. Everything was lost in the blast. I have to meet with the banks and Rob's firm. I will be there with you in a few days. Please pray.

My mom is calling. Let me tell her what has happened. I will call you back."

Rob had been the most wonderful son, brother, and uncle to his nieces and nephews. He would be present for their games and events as much as possible. He was very supportive and had taken care of his mom after his father had passed away. He was nearly perfect in every way it seemed. This was a devastating loss for their family and Vivian's; as he was supportive of her family also.

"Hi, Mom."

"Vivian... what is going on in Chicago? I just called to make sure you and my son-in-law are okay."

"No mom. We are not okay. Rob was killed this morning in an explosion that took place in our building after we were asked to evacuate the condo. He went back in to get some things we had forgotten; then the building exploded and went up in flames. He didn't make it." Vivian began sobbing again.

"Vivian, listen honey. You need to come home."

"Mom, I can't come right now. I have to sort some things out here and then meet with his firm before I go to Atlanta to make the arrangements for the memorial."

"Okay Vivian. But as soon as you can. You need to come home."

A DIVINE TWIST OF FATE

There was something about her mother's words that resonated within her. Why was she so adamant that I come home right now? Especially since this just occurred. Vivian repeated her mom's words over and over and they seemed to pierce her thoughts. This was unusual for her mother to insist on her coming home. But nonetheless, she promised her mom that as soon as she could, she would take a flight to Greenville before going to Atlanta.

Vivian did not know how she was going to get any rest. She made a few more calls, ordered some food from the hotel restaurant, and went up to her hotel room to shower and change into some more comfortable clothing.

Her mind was still all over the place.

She didn't want to see or hear the news. People knew who she was because she and Rob were immersed deep into the community and led high profile careers. The hotel attendants were cautious to not allow any media to bother her and she asked them to hold calls of anyone searching for her.

She just wanted quiet.

Through tears, Vivian whispered, "Lord. I know that I have not done everything you have wanted me to do. I have not been to church in so long and I've not been faithful in my relationship with you. I just don't understand though, why Rob? Why did you allow this to happen to us?"

In her heart, she didn't really anticipate that God would respond because she hadn't talked to Him in so long. Yet, she didn't know where else to turn at this point. She just wanted answers.

The only things she had left were the cars and the items that she and Rob brought out of the condo. Of course, there was money in the bank accounts, as well as a cottage in the Hamptons, the boat, and the beach house in Emerald Isle, but there were no memories. They were all gone. All of their pictures, art, her crafts (she was a craft designer in her spare time), the piano – everything was gone.

Vivian looked around the hotel room, crying and trying to make sense of everything that had occurred in the last 24 hours. She could afford the finest things in life, but the one thing she wanted right now was her husband to come walking through those doors.

A DIVINE TWIST OF FATE

She just wanted her precious Rob back.

After soaking in the tub for a few hours, while listening to some instrumental music, Vivian drifted off to sleep.

She then heard a buzzing that woke her back up. It was her phone. Looking at the screen, she didn't recognize the number, but decided to answer it anyway.

"Hello, this is Vivian."

On the other end was a voice that she had never heard before. A voice that would dismantle her world even further. It was a gentleman.

"Hi Ms. Vivian... I know you don't know me, but I just wanted to call and express my condolences to you."

"Who is this?"

"Ms. Vivian... this is Rob's son, Xavier."

"Son? My husband did not have any children. You must have the wrong number. Please do not call me again."

"Wait! Ms. Vivian, please don't hang up. I can prove who I am. Please. Will you meet with me?"

"No! This is a hoax. I don't believe you! How did you get this number? Who are you? You just want money from me! Please leave me alone. How dare you call me while I am grieving over the loss of my husband! He wouldn't do that to me. He would have told me."

"Ms. Vivian, I assure you. I don't want money. My dad took very good care of me and my sisters."

"Sisters... What do you mean sisters? What are you talking about? My Rob did not have any children. My God! This is not happening to me."

"Ms. Vivian... please will you meet with me? I think that will be better."

"Okay. Okay." Through tears, Vivian decided to meet with the young man. "Let's meet tomorrow near the Harris Theater at Millennium Park at noon. I have to meet with my husband's firm and the banks tomorrow, as well as the attorney handling his affairs."

"Okay, Ms. Vivian. I will be there at noon with one of my sisters, Kiersten."

Her night just got worse. She could not believe what she had just heard. Children... Rob has children? I thought he never wanted children. *No! There's no way. This is a joke and it is going to come to an end tomorrow.*

"God! Why didn't you tell me about this? Why didn't you show me that Rob was a cheater? Why didn't you tell me about his infidelity? Why did you let this happen to me God? Please tell me why you let this happen to me?"

Vivian did not even want to discuss this with anyone until she had proof. So, she called a friend of hers who was also a private detective. She never had to use his services before because she always trusted Rob, but now she needed some answers.

"Hello."

"Tim. This is Vivian. How are you?"

"I am doing well Vivian. How are you?"

"I have been better. Did you hear about the explosion in Chicago?"

"Yes, how awful."

"Tim... That was our building. We lived on the penthouse floor. I am okay, but Rob was killed in the explosion."

"Vivian... I am so sorry to hear that. You have my prayers and condolences."

"Thank you Tim. Listen, the reason I called is that I need a favor. Money is no issue. I just received the most disturbing phone call from a young man claiming to be Rob's son. He said that his name is Xavier. I need some answers. I never had a reason to distrust Rob until now.

Can you help me?"

Tim replied, "Yes. I can help. I just need some information from you."

"I am meeting Xavier tomorrow at noon in front of the Millennium Park at Harris Theater. Can you be there also?"

"Yes, I can watch from a distance, and then meet with you afterward."

"Okay. Thank you. I am staying at a hotel downtown until I get the legal matters and bank paperwork sorted out, as well as meeting with his firm. I will speak with you tomorrow, Vivian said, before hanging up the phone.

She felt uneasy, but calmer. She just could not fathom Rob lying to her about not one child, but three. This was a nightmare getting worse. She took some pain medicine for the migraine which was forming and decided to lie down.

The last 24 hours seemed like a never-ending bad dream.

Bzzzz...

The next morning her alarm went off.

She pressed the remote for the curtains to open and the sun was rising over the water. As she looked out the window, she hoped for a moment that she had been dreaming.

Turning to look toward the other side of the bed... no Rob. She still could not believe what was happening in her life right now. What was God trying to tell her?

She remembered the words from her favorite childhood novel, *Are you there God? It's me Margaret*. She whispered, "Are you there God? It's me Vivian. I need you right now. Please."

Silence. She heard nothing from God.

She wanted to call her mother and Liz and tell them everything, but she couldn't. She felt so humiliated and angry.

Now she was angry with Rob.

Although she was upset that he was gone, she was angry that he lied to her. She was angry about all of this secrecy and infidelity. Why? Why did he have to do this to her? He didn't have to lie. He could have just left.

Her mind was racing. She calmed herself down and decided to wait to hear what Xavier and his sister had to say before drawing any conclusions.

She got dressed. She knew she was going to have to go shopping at some point, because she had lost all of her clothing and shoes in the explosion. Yet, she had managed to get a few things packed into a bag. She pulled herself together, put on some makeup attempting to hide all of the tears and weariness in her face, then she went downstairs.

There was a package waiting for her at the desk. How did anyone know she was here? The doorman said it was delivered late the night before by a gentleman who was clean dressed and said he had something for her.

This was getting scarier and spookier by the minute. No one, at least she thought no one knew she had checked into the hotel. She had even used cash to pay for the room, instead of her cards.

She wasn't ready to open the package, because she was almost afraid to know the contents. She wanted to meet with

Xavier first. And then meet with Tim to begin making sense of all of this.

She arrived at her destination and began looking for this young man who claimed to be her husband's son. She had sent him a picture of herself and he responded with one as well. Of course, he already knew what she looked like because he had been in Rob's life for many years and Rob had advised Xavier to reach out to Vivian if anything ever happened to him.

Xavier approached from the east side of the fountain; with his younger sister, Kiersten. Vivian recognized him right away. He was a handsome young man, and looked so much like Rob, it was undeniable that this was his son.

She gasped, because now she knew that he wasn't lying. His eyes were just as deep and mesmerizing, even the way he wore his hair and his style of dress. His walk was distinctly Rob.

But how? How did this happen? When?

Tears formed in Vivian's eyes as he and his sister came closer. She looked a lot like Rob as well. Quickly Vivian whispered a prayer, "Father please help me. This can't be happening. Please help me."

Xavier walked up and shook Vivian's hand, "Greetings, Ms. Vivian. Nice to finally meet you. This is my younger sister Kiersten."

Vivian greeted them both and they sat down. She had brought them some lunch and they all sat and talked. Vivian stated, "I don't even know where to begin. This is all very overwhelming for me and I am deeply hurt by this situation."

Xavier responded, "Ms. Vivian. I understand. Our dad stated that you were a wonderful woman, and that you would be shocked, but understanding of everything. Our mother was not supportive of this meeting, but we told her that it is what our dad would have wanted."

Vivian, still in shock, and tears flowing responded, "But why? Why did he do this to me? Is this why he never wanted to have children with me? I am so devastated by this. With his death and I can't ask him any questions. And you... it's just all too much. Did any of his family know about this?"

Kiersten replied, "Yes Ms. Vivian. We have met all of his family."

"Oh my God. And no one told me. No one in his family thought enough of me to tell me?"

Xavier replied, "Ms. Vivian. We are so sorry. Our grandmother and uncles told him to tell you numerous times. He just brushed it off. He loved you, but he said that he wasn't happy."

Vivian thought, "How dare these strangers come in and tell her about her marriage and relationship with the most wonderful man she had ever known?!" Then she began to remember the nights when he said he was tired, and had long days and couldn't spend time with her, because he was so busy with work. She started calculating, as she listened to Xavier share about their experiences with Rob and how all of this came about, how their mom moved from Atlanta to Chicago when Xavier was born.

Then she remembered when Rob first came to her and said, "Let's move to Chicago, Viv."

She said aloud, "He had gotten a job with the firm and found the penthouse apartment and we packed our Atlanta lives up and moved here. But, the only reason he really came here was because of your mother and you."

Did everyone know about this except me?

"Xavier you're 21 and Kiersten 15? So for the 15 years they lived in Chicago, Rob had this affair with your mother; which also means the affair began not long after he and I got married 23 years ago."

Tears flowed down her face. She couldn't believe this man that she shared life with all these years had been cheating on her the entire time. She had missed it. She had trusted him implicitly. How? How did he manage it?

She questioned everything up through this moment. She questioned every time Rob ever said he loved her. She began thinking about the late meetings, the late phone calls, the conferences he said he had to attend, the out of town clients, the shopping trips to other countries, and the beach house trips without her.

Had he taken these strangers, this other woman and her children, to the places that were supposed to be sacred between them? Everything was a lie. It was all one big lie.

The extravagant wedding they had, the honeymoon. All of that was a lie. Why? Why did he marry her then?

"Ms. Vivian? Ms. Vivian..."

"Yes, what did you say? I'm sorry. My mind is just overwhelmed with all of this."

"We are sorry Ms. Vivian, we know this is a lot to absorb. We would love to spend more time with you and just really share things with you concerning the relationship with our dad. We promise we do not want anything from you other than to have a relationship with you because of him. He provided for us and we have trust funds that will take care of us until we are 30. We do not need anything. He took very good care of our mother as well."

Vivian began thinking again, *It was as if these people are throwing salt in my open wounds.* Are they serious? Can they really believe that this is okay? That I even want a relationship with them?"

"Xavier and Kiersten. The two of you are beautiful kids and I see my husband in both of you. But I can't do this. I am sorry. I need some time. Please."

Xavier replied, "Sure Ms. Vivian. We do understand. We were just really hoping to get to know you because of our dad. We would really like to be included in the arrangements for his service."

Vivian stated, "Of course. I will make sure you are included. I'd really like to meet with your mother as well. I need some time to process all of this. Please just let me get through the services, the will, and legal matters before we meet again. I will be in touch."

"Sure Ms. Vivian. Sure. We understand and we just want you to know that we are here. We are saddened by his death, yet he spent as much time with us as he could. He loved us very well."

"Okay Xavier and Kiersten. I would like to say it has been a pleasure meeting you, but I honestly do not know how I feel right now. I am numb. I loved your father, but clearly he did not love me. It will truly take me some time to get through this. I have to go home to Greenville, SC and I must go meet with Rob's family. I will be in touch with you."

"Thank you for meeting with us Ms. Vivian. Please let us know if there is anything we can do to assist you with the arrangements."

Vivian walked back to her car.

"Wow," Vivian thought. She could not believe all of this. It was as if these children knew everything about her, but she knew nothing of them. Rob was going to leave and she had no idea. How could she have missed all of this? She had been living a fantasy all this time.

Immediately after getting in the car, she phoned Tim and told him everything she had just learned. Tim advised that he would do some digging and research, even check in with the firm to get as much information as possible, and report back to her in a few days.

Then she called her mother. She explained everything to her mom, who stated, "I am not surprised baby girl. This is why I told you that you need to come home. I have wanted to talk to you for years, but you never seemed to sit still long enough or make the time for me to share what was on my heart. The Lord had shown me years ago that there were things going on with Rob that didn't add up, and every time I would attempt to talk to you, you would tell me that you did not have time or you had somewhere to go. Now you are going to listen. Come home Vivian. Just come home."

"Okay mom. I am coming. I have my flight booked. I just need to meet with the firm and the attorneys handling the will and estate. I will be there in a few days."

There were going to be two memorials. One in Chicago and one in Atlanta. She wanted to do the one in Atlanta first and then fly back to Chicago to hold the second one.

Then there was this mysterious package she received. She arrived back to the hotel and told herself that she would open it once she got to the room. She checked in with the desk and there were no messages or packages for her. She went to the room, ordered room service from the hotel restaurant, and began to unwind from this outlandish day.

She was still in shock by the things Xavier and Kiersten shared with her. Rob had been unfaithful their entire marriage. And what was just as bad was his family knew and no one told her. *Not one person in his family thought enough of me to tell me what was going on*, she thought.

Not one.

Vivian sat down on the bed and began to open the package. The box was nicely wrapped in colorful paper. There was a plain off-white envelope on the top of the contents. She opened the letter and began reading.

She could not believe the words on the paper:

A DIVINE TWIST OF FATE

Greetings Mrs. Challis,

You do not know me, but my name is Charles, and I apologize for the circumstances under which you are receiving this letter. I heard of your husband's passing and I wanted to reach out to you because I think it is important that we meet. Rob was involved with my wife. I worked with him at the firm and my wife had some legal matters and I referred her to him. I followed them for years. The pictures are included in this package. At first, I thought he was just helping her as an attorney, because I made the referral, but I soon found out that they were having a very intense affair that went on for about three years.

"Oh my God, Vivian gasped. She could not believe what she was reading, yet she continued.

I know this comes as a shock to you. I have wanted to share this with you for numerous years; however, the time never seemed to be right. I watched you as you supported him at every event, how you were the loving and faithful wife, while he was out here doing whatever he wanted to do. I wanted her to tell me the truth, but she never did. I didn't press it with her, because at the time, I had some medical concerns that kept me from being the husband she needed me to be.

Shortly after I found out about the affair, I confronted him, and left the firm. It was either I leave, or they were going to fire me, based on his position within the company. My wife was in a terrible accident, not long after I confronted him, and she died. It was then that I found out she was not the only woman he had been messing around with. He also has two children, Xavier and Kiersten. He had still been involved with their mother, until the day he was killed in that awful explosion.

I saw the news, where it mentioned him dying, and decided to contact you. After my wife died in the accident, I became obsessed with destroying Rob's life, because he had destroyed mine, but then God intervened and redirected my path. Since that time, I have been ministering and assisting couples who find themselves caught in adultery, lies, and deception.

My heart's desire is to save as many marriages as God will allow, so that families can be restored.
Vivian, I truly apologize for having to share this information with you. There was a child involved. My wife had a baby, a son. She was pregnant by Rob, and I told her that I would help her through the process, and not leave until after the child was born.

Two weeks after she gave birth, she was killed in the car accident. I have been caring for him as though he were my own because I refused to allow Rob to have access to his life.

It's the only part of her I have left.

So I guess we both have suffered tremendous loss. My prayer is to sit down with you face-to-face and share more with you; maybe to help you make sense of all of this, because it is truly tragic.

Please feel free to call me once you have read this letter and reviewed the contents of the package. My number is listed below.

Thank you for taking the time to read this and hopefully I will hear from you soon.

Sincerely,
Charles Redmon

"Can my life get any worse?" Vivian thought. "A man exclaiming that my beloved Rob had an affair with his wife. When will this horrible nightmare end?"

It was getting late but she wanted to share this bit of information with Tim. She called and he was not available so she left a message... "Tim, this is Vivian. Call me as soon as possible. Something else has happened, you are not going to believe it and I need your help.

Thanks."

She rummaged through the box. There she saw pictures of the child, now 19 years old, and of Charles' wife and Rob together at numerous, yet familiar places.

Still crying, she replayed the last 23 years of her life all over again. *Rob was so unfaithful to me, even though I was faithful to him. I could have been anywhere with anyone. I gave up the man who really loved me so that I could be with Rob and I turned my back on God's purpose for my life.* "Lord, can you ever forgive me?" Vivian remembered the words Mr. Redmon wrote. He mentioned that he was so angry with Rob that he wanted to destroy his life, but God intervened. "What an amazing act of forgiveness on his part. How in the world could he possibly forgive his wife or Rob? I cannot even fathom forgiving Rob or either of these women. My heart just can't understand how Rob could do this to me."

Just then a song came on the music channel. She didn't even remember turning on the television, but must have so that she could unwind. The words resonated in her ears,

"No weapon formed against me, shall prosper.
It won't work. God will do what He said he would do,
He will stand by His word. He will come through."

For the first time in her life, she felt the presence of the Holy Spirit around her. It was as if God was saying to her, "I have this under control. Don't worry."

Vivian had never had this experience before. She had never been touched by God's presence. He was there in the room with her. Tears filled her eyes and an overwhelming feeling of love filled her heart. She knew that she had to do the right things despite Rob's lies, deception and infidelity.

She knew that she had to take the higher road.

At that moment, she knew that God was with her.

Had he allowed all of this to occur in her life just so that she could acknowledge Him once again? She had forgotten about God. Every time she would come close, she would run, because she wanted to do things her way, instead of His way.

But this time, He had her right where He wanted her... in His presence. She sat there, tears falling from her eyes and just began to worship in her own way "Father thank you for loving me in spite of myself. Thank you for giving me another chance. You are so worthy!"

Through tears and sobs, she just worshipped God.

She thought about all of the times she had rejected Him and went her own way; how she chose this life with Rob over being a praise and worship leader at church (yes she had an amazingly anointed and beautiful voice), and being a minister. She had been told that she had a powerful women's and children's ministry, yet she rejected this because she wanted live a lavish life and Rob had swept her off her feet; making promise after promise that he was going to be the greatest thing that ever happened to her... and he was until now. Until this moment when she was face to face with her Creator.

She surrendered her will.

Vivian cried like she had never cried before, until finally she drifted off to sleep.

The next morning, she called Mr. Redmond. Her voice was very shaky, but she wanted to make things right, if she could. None of this was her fault; nevertheless, she felt responsible because after all, this was Rob's child that Mr. Redmon was raising.

Plus Xavier and Kiersten needed to know that they had a brother.

"Hello." She heard Mr. Redmon's voice on the other end of the phone.

"Mr. Redmon. This is Vivian Challis. I was hoping that we could meet today or tomorrow. Is your schedule free?"

"Sure. Where would you like to meet?"

"Is it possible for you to meet me at the coffee shop near Rob's office?

"Sure. I can do that? What time?"

"At 12:30 today, if possible?"

"Sure, I will be there."

Vivian hung up the phone.

Charles had placed a picture of both he and his wife in the box as well, so Vivian knew who to look for.

It was almost 12:30 pm. Here was the next moment of truth. Vivian pulled up in front of the coffee shop and went inside to get a table. She was a little early, so she ordered a coffee and pastry. She waited patiently and looked towards the window facing the river.

She still could not believe what her life had come to. Gazing out the window, she nearly became lost in the ambiance of the beautiful day.

"Mrs. Challis."

She heard this amazing voice behind her. "It's Charles." She looked up and the man standing in front of her was tall, dressed very nicely, and absolutely gorgeous; just a little more seasoned than she expected.

She had to catch her thoughts. He still looked the same as in the photo, just older. "What woman could have possibly wanted to mistreat him or cheat on him? She must have been a fool. Even though Rob was just as handsome. She still must have been a fool to cheat on her husband," she thought.

"Hi Mr. Redmon. Nice to meet you. Please... call me Vivian."

"Nice to meet you as well Vivian. Please do not get up. You're the lady." He nicely and firmly shook her hand without squeezing too hard, and looked her straight in the eyes.

"Wow what a gentleman," she thought. "Charles, I was a few minutes early, so I ordered a coffee and pastry. If you'd like to order something, please do."

"Thank you. I will just get some coffee. I had breakfast, so I'm not very hungry right now. I'll be right back Ms. Vivian."

Vivian was baffled. This man was a perfect gentleman. She could not imagine any woman wanting to leave him. Yet, she was reminded of how lust really worked, obviously because there was nothing but lust between her and Rob. There could not have been a foundation of love or else he would not have done all of these horrible things.

Perfect love casts out fear. Love covers a multitude of sins.

"Huh? What was that? Did I just hear that in my head?"

I said, "Perfect love casts out fear. Love covers a multitude of sins. My perfect love overcomes all of these things you are now experiencing Vivian. You do not have to harbor un-forgiveness, or think poorly of anyone. It is upon me to judge them, not you."

"Wow!" For the first time in years, she heard the voice of God speaking to her. It was absolutely amazing. She thought she was losing it. In those few minutes, waiting for Charles to return, she clearly heard the Holy Spirit speak to her about forgiveness.

Her heart was broken and heavy, still she felt lighter than days before.

Charles returned to the table and they began conversing about everything that had happened; back then and in the last few days. She was astonished by the level of spiritual insight, maturity, and forgiveness with which this man spoke.

Something inside of her was changing, but she did not allow it to show. She was feeling the weight of this burden lift from her. She knew what she had to do. She knew she still had to have Rob's memorial services, and meet with the families, Rob's children, his friends, and his colleagues.

She knew that she had to listen to the reading of his Will, but the daunting heaviness of it all was dissipating.

She felt so much lighter.

"Vivian..." Charles paused. "My wife was beautiful and I could have never imagined anyone else being with her except me, but she never loved me. She was always the one to party and hang out with her girlfriends while I was at home. I would have never done anything to hurt her, which is why I refused to allow anyone else to raise her son. But your husband must have been a fool to leave you for her or anyone else. You are absolutely an amazing woman."

A DIVINE TWIST OF FATE

"Thank you Charles. That is very kind of you to say. Honestly, I thought the same thing about your wife. How she must have been a fool to leave you for anyone else, including my husband; as charming and handsome as he was.

Truly I am sorry that all of this happened in your life Charles. No one deserves to be treated this way."

"You're right Ms. Vivian. You didn't deserve this level of pain either. However, I truly believe that God allowed all of this to work for our good. Through this experience, I came back to God and began to fulfill my purpose. I am not sure what all of this will mean for you, but from listening to you, it sounds as if you have been experiencing some encounters with God through this as well, is that right?"

"Yes Charles. In fact, I had turned my back on God years ago to follow Rob and his dreams; to live this phenomenal and lavish life here in the city, only to be brought back to nothing. Everything we owned, except the other properties and some money in the bank, was in that condo. Sure material possessions, such as houses and cars can be replaced, but pictures and all of the unique artifacts and things we collected over the years cannot.

In my younger years, I would sing praises and worship God, attend church regularly and faithfully, but I gave all of that up when I married Rob. Somehow, I had convinced myself that he loved God too, but over the years, as we traveled more and purchased properties, we stopped attending services.

We stopped praying together, even though we didn't pray together often; we would from time to time. All of that ceased after just a few short years. Now that I think about it, and reminisce on the earlier years, I can see all of the gaps in time where Rob was away. He provided reasons which seemed legitimate for his absences, but now it all makes sense. He was having multiple affairs.

Who is to say that there aren't more women out there who he was involved with?"

"Ms. Vivian, I totally understand how you feel. He was a very wealthy man as well. He had other properties that you don't know about and he made millions of dollars as an attorney defending people from all walks of life. Maybe now you will truly be able to make good use of what he left you."

"Sounds like you know more about him than I do Charles."

"Vivian, I worked very closely with your husband. I know about every deal made and every purchase he ever made while I was there. I had even hired a private detective to spy on him and my wife, so I would have the proof I needed to destroy him, but I was never able to get that far. I have spent the last 19 years raising her son and ministering to couples and the community.

Would you like to visit a service sometime?"

"Sure Charles. That would be nice. Perhaps we should keep in touch. Especially, since now I have to have some sort of relationship with Xavier and Kiersten. They need to meet their brother. I can arrange for that to take place. I also plan to meet with their mother. I really need to hear what she has to say."

"Rob left a property for her and the kids. Maybe we can drive there to meet and speak with her. I think we both owe it to ourselves to get more closure on this, so we can move forward with our lives."

"Sure Charles. That would be great. I am planning to go to Greenville and Atlanta in a couple of days to meet with his family, so perhaps we need to meet her before I do that. Especially, since she may be at Rob's memorial. Truly I am sorry to hear about your wife, but you are a caring and loving person to be a father to her son. Are you going to talk to him about Rob?"

"I did. A few years ago. After I explained it to him, he said that he didn't want to meet him. I just told him about the explosion, so he wants to come to the memorial just to see who this man was. Well, thank you for taking the time to meet with me. If you will reach out to Xavier or Kiersten and let them know what is going on, I will make arrangements to drive you there."

"Thanks so much Charles for sharing everything with me, I can see how difficult it was for you all of these years. I will make sure that you and Keith are well taken care of afterwards, since you have sacrificed so much of your life and financial resources; even losing your job behind all of this. I am not sure how I will ever recover from this, yet I now realize that God is with me, and has been this entire time. I have to meet with the attorneys and the firm tomorrow, so I will call you once that is done."

"God has never left or forsaken you, Vivian. Even though it may seem like it. And I've learned there is nothing that we can do to be separated from His love. He loves you and He is causing everything to work together for your good. His ways are not our ways and He knew all of this would happen to bring us to this place. His will and purpose are divine.

Your destiny in His hands. It is up to you to receive His love and follow the path He has for you now; to be obedient to the call He has on your life."

What an amazing conversation, she whispered. Vivian believed, at this point, that she could move forward, despite the brokenness and grief she felt. The days to come would be challenging, but she knew she could make it. She knew that she shouldn't feel this way, yet somehow she and Charles connected in a way she had not intended.

There was something sacred about the meeting, something she pondered in her heart from the moment she left his presence. She believes he felt it also. Only God knows what had transpired in those moments.

Charles spoke to her spirit, something she had not known before. He left an ineffaceable mark upon her soul.

The next day Vivian met with Rob's colleagues at the firm. She was appalled by the things she learned, but did her best to honor Rob's life and work within the community; focusing on moving forward, so that she could get the memorials out of the way.

She met with the attorney concerning Rob's will. He left her everything that they had together (the houses, bank accounts, investments) of course, and had also set up a renewable trust for her to establish her own publishing company, as well as her non-profit art gallery.

He knew that Vivian loved art and wanted to ensure that she was able to realize her dreams. She was surprised because for all of the years that she told him she wanted to have her own publishing company, it was as if he really didn't listen to her. He loved art as well, but never seemed to be interested in owning a gallery.

The attorney disclosed that Rob had also left quite a bit to his children and their mother.

Why wasn't she surprised? After everything that happened over the last two weeks, this was not really a shock to her.

Vivian and Charles met the next day to drive and speak with Xavier and Kiersten's mother.

When they arrived, they were blown away by the magnitude of the home. She had lived well off of Vivian's husband.

How dare she?

Vivian was nervous, but Charles assured her that he would be right there to help her through the process.

Kristene was a beautiful woman; in her mid-50s, she had obviously aged gracefully. Right away, she apologized to Vivian for what she had done, admitting that she knew Rob was married and didn't care.

LADY ANGEL MILLER

"He loved me first and that's all I wanted, but when he didn't marry me, I told him that I would never let him see Xavier if he didn't take care of us financially. I was so angry with him for marrying you, and I wanted you to hurt, but I know it wasn't your fault. It was him... and even though I knew it was him, I wasn't willing to let him go.

When I saw on the news that he had died in that explosion, part of me was relieved, but I know that isn't right. I just was so angry with him for marrying you. For many years, I wanted to confront you, but he told me if I ever did that he would sue me for custody of the children and make my life miserable.

I didn't believe him at first, but once he cancelled my bank accounts, and told me that he would take the house.

So, I kept quiet and allowed things to continue. I am so sorry Mrs. Challis. Woman to woman, I should have done the right thing, regardless of how much money and stuff he flashed in our faces. The kids don't know that side of him. They don't know how ruthless he could be and I guess you don't really know either. I am so sorry you had to find out about your husband this way."

Tears streamed down Vivian's face and she was angry. She felt resentment creeping in, yet she fought the thoughts. She wanted to scream at her, but she couldn't.

She was numb.

Instead, Vivian just cried and shook her head in disbelief. All she could think about was the many times Rob had apparently lied to her about his whereabouts.

"Kristene, we hate to tell you this, but you weren't the only one Rob was having an affair with. He was also having an affair with Charles' wife and she was pregnant with Rob's child as well. His name is Keith. She was killed in a car accident not long after Keith was born. We want him to meet Kiersten and Xavier before the memorial. Is that okay with you?"

Kristene responded, "Of course. I am not surprised. He had always been a ladies man from what I knew of him. I am sad that he is gone, but honestly, it got to the point that I no longer loved him. He was really around for the kids."

"Thank you for taking the time to talk with us. I will make sure that Xavier and Kiersten connect with Keith," stated Charles. "He is a great kid."

Vivian didn't say much during the drive back to the city. Charles was a perfect gentleman and just allowed some soft instrumental music to fill the silence. She rehearsed everything in her head and just wanted to prepare her mind for the trip home to Atlanta over the next few days.

Charles offered to drive her to the airport in the morning and she accepted.

At the Chicago airport, the news continued to show scenes from the accident. It was all she could do to fight the tears. She boarded the plane and prayed silently along the way. The flight was calming and memories continued to flood her mind.

Captivated in her thoughts, she almost missed the stewardess saying they had arrived safely in Greenville.

Liz met her at the airport and they were able to catch up. She disclosed everything to Liz; they both cried because Liz and her husband loved Rob as though he were their brother.

His actions were unbelievable, but now he was gone, so there was no way to confront him about his behavior.

Vivian's parents had always loved Rob and treated him as family. Her mom held her tightly and assured her that everything would be alright.

She just wanted to ensure that her baby girl was okay.

Her parents drove her to Atlanta to attend the memorial. Vivian didn't have the strength to address Rob's family or ask them why they had condoned his behavior. She just wanted to get it over with and honor her husband in a way that she knew would please God. She knew that she had to forgive all of them; in spite of the pain caused.

Xavier, Kiersten, their mother, and Keith were in attendance. Vivian assured Charles that she would look after Keith.

During the service, the pastor spoke about forgiveness. Was he speaking directly to Vivian? It was as if his message was just for her.

She knew that God was with her, even in this.

The grief was overwhelming, but there was also a great deal of healing that took place. Rob's family apologized to

Vivian over and over; however, she was unable to process anything they said to her in those moments. She left them the checks that Rob wanted them to have, one for his parents, siblings, nieces and nephews.

Vivian also wrote a check to Keith from her private account. She had promised Charles that she would take care of them. She told him not to open it until he got home to his dad; he hugged her and agreed.

Finally she could breathe.

So much had happened, she forgot about the assignment she gave Tim. She called him to let him know that she would meet with him when she returned to Chicago. This would be the last step of her closure.

Before Vivian boarded the plane back to Chicago, she hugged and said goodbye to her family and Liz. Her parents agreed to stay in town for a few days to help Rob's family through the transition.

Vivian could not bring herself to stay.

The flight home was peaceful, and she knew in those few moments, that her life was going to be better and she was about to embark upon a new beginning.

A DIVINE TWIST OF FATE

She took a deep breath, cried and whispered *"Thank you Lord for my divine purpose and this next phase of my life. I trust you and I will do what you have called me to do. Thank you for this second chance and I receive everything you have for me. Thank you."*

In her heart, she knew this was a new beginning and could not wait to see Charles to share how the service went and her thoughts about moving forward. She finally felt free and knew that unconditional and pure love was on the horizon.

About the Authors

DR. JOY LOUGH, PhD is an Author, Motivational Speaker, Consultant and Educator. With over 20 years of experience in entrepreneurship, business, and human resources, she is the CEO of Joy Lough Enterprises, LLC.

Their mission is to IMPACT lives professionally and personally through education, motivation, and inspiration.

Dr. Joy assists entrepreneurs with the startup and development of their organizations and provides personal development for individuals. Dr. Joy is passionate about helping build and foster productive and prosperous members of society.

Dr. Joy has spoken and lectured at schools, colleges, universities, churches, and community events in a variety of venues.

For booking or more information: **www.joylough.com**